Bill Gauthier

Alice on the Shelf

For
Michelle Marshall,
who knows why.
&
For
Toby Gray,
who helped me through.

For two friends, this tale of doubles.

"Thy loving smile will surely hail
The love-gift of a fairy-tale."

—Lewis Carroll
Through the Looking Glass

I

LATE NIGHT FEARS & A DRIVE

Where's Alice? was Brad's first thought when his eyes popped open at 2 AM. Strangely, it wasn't Alice he saw in his mind's eye—for he knew no one named Alice—but instead his friend Miranda. Her dark red hair, her pointed eyebrows over crystal blue, ever-knowing eyes, her Cheshire Cat smile. It made sense. She *loved* Lewis Carroll's *Alice* books.

His first thought was immediately followed by, *She needs help.*

Though he believed his imagination was playing with him, the idea that Miranda was in trouble lingered, wriggling into every fiber of his guts and his heart.

At 2:05 AM, Brad threw off his sheets and got out of bed. His hands trembled as he grabbed the phone. His mind screamed, *What the hell are you doing?* Miranda wouldn't like getting a frantic phone call at five-past-two in the morning just to make sure she was all right.

Brad put the phone down. His right hand went to rub his wedding band. It wasn't there of course, hadn't been for a couple of months now. And still, Miranda didn't seem interested in taking their friendship further. Yet. He went to the refrigerator and poured himself a glass of white grape peach juice. He sat on the couch. Dull yellow light from the streetlamps outside slid between the blinds' slats but the white light of the full moon came in stronger, throwing Brad's shadow on the floor in the small, dark living room. His bachelor pad, he mused. Brad looked at the clock on the cable box. 2:09 AM. In the dark, the shape of his sleeping notebook computer taunted him. He'd tried writing tonight before finally giving up and going to bed. For some reason, the words wouldn't come. Perhaps they were trapped in his heart?

His heart. Even as the thick, sweet juice coated his tongue like liquid silk and rolled down his throat, his heart raced. Miranda was in trouble.

He didn't want to call her. *If* nothing was wrong—and that was the probability—then he'd seem crazy. Still, all the rationalizing in the world wouldn't drive the sense of trouble away from him. If he just knew she was all right...

Maybe a quick drive would ease your fears, a voice suggested. It was his voice but a little deeper, more secure in itself. It was the voice that often told him what to write.

The nervous energy, while not disappearing, eased a bit. A drive sounded good. Brad finished his juice, threw on jeans, and grabbed his jacket. At the least, the fresh air would be good for him.

He drove aimlessly, mindful of the happenings around him if not his surroundings. If something out of the ordinary happened, he'd be fine. But what was ordinary on a night like this?

Brad didn't realize where his subconscious had led him until he turned onto South Andrade Road. His heart sank with guilt. Sometimes it felt as though his own mind was fucking with him. South Andrade Road. The street where Miranda lived.

Why not? the voice asked. *You're concerned about your friend.*

Upon thinking of Miranda, the surety that she was in trouble returned. It was insane, of course—paranoia—but he still couldn't stop the dreadful feeling as he pulled to the curb.

Miranda rented a small house that she'd shared with her boyfriend until a month ago. Inside were two small bedrooms, a living room, an eat-in kitchen, and a bathroom. The front porch was screened in and she and Brad had sat on it a few times, talking, sipping tea, Miranda smoking a cigarette. They talked about books (they had several favorite writers in common) movies (they both loved horror movies and *Star Wars*) philosophies (there were many) and dreams (he wanted to write, she wanted...happiness). She, like his best friend Tommy, who lived with his wife and young son in New Hampshire, was one of the few people Brad had ever met with whom he had so much in common, including his ex-wife Karen. Their relationship had been easy and comfortable from the start. Except for—

He stopped his thoughts from going down that road. *That* couldn't happen. Miranda had drawn the line, and though he hoped the line was in the sand and could someday be washed away by the tide, it remained a line that he'd respect. Everyone could use a friend.

The full moon dropped a blue-white blanket on the house and surrounding bushes. The lights were off. If anything were happening, one couldn't see it from the outside.

Then go inside, the voice said. There was something about it that chilled Brad.

Brad realized how preposterous this whole thing was.

He sat looking at himself from a distance. At almost three in the morning he was in his car outside his friend's house because a dream he couldn't remember had convinced him that something bad was happening to her. It was fucked-up, no other term for it.

And it wasn't even Miranda, he told himself. *It was* Alice.

The specifics didn't matter because the whole thing was ridiculous. It was insane that the same imagination that allowed him to produce fiction would intrude on his real life in such a way. It had been an issue during his three years of marriage to Karen. How many panic attacks had they sat through together? Wasn't the very fact that he married her a sign of his fears? At the age of twenty-three, he hadn't the confidence to believe anyone else would ever want him. He and Karen had been together since his senior year of high school (she'd been a year behind) and marriage seemed like the safest bet. Never mind his feelings that he was settling, that they would both be happier with other people. He too easily pictured himself alone and so had agreed to marry her. And that's how it had been, too, he'd agreed. He remembered the day at their new apartment. He'd sat in front of the computer, working on a novel that had never gone anywhere except the proverbial writer's trunk, and she'd told him they'd be married next year. And there he was the following year, reminding himself that he was lucky that *anyone* would want him.

It wasn't until he'd met Miranda that he realized just how wrong he'd been on so many fronts.

Brad was about to turn the key and restart the ignition, promising himself he'd call Tommy in the morning for a verbal smack in the head, when the bushes on the side of Miranda's house moved. The hairs tingled on the back of his neck. It had to be the wind. Despite the cool September air, there was no wind tonight. A cool breeze came through the half open driver's side window and barely ruffled his hair. Tonight there was no wind strong enough to rattle the shrubs like *that*.

He stared at the bushes for several beats.

Your imagination, he told himself and began to turn the key, when the bushes moved again. This time, he knew he wasn't seeing things.

Brad got out of the car and the cool air bit at him. He closed the door, hoping the noise wouldn't awaken Miranda's neighbors, and slowly approached her house. The bushes rattled again and this time he saw something. It looked light blue under the full moon but was most likely white; not the usual dark colors one chose to blend in with the night.

He realized he didn't have anything to protect himself with. If this guy had a weapon, Brad was fucked. Unlike Tommy, he knew no martial arts. He quickly scanned the ground for something—anything—that might help. A glitter in the grass caught his eye. A rock or an equally heavy object, he hoped.

He grabbed it and knew immediately it wasn't a rock. It fit in the palm of his hand and was heavy, made of cold metal. Ticking in his hand was a large pocket watch from which hung a gold chain. The time was accurate with the large hand pointing between the XI and the XII and the small hand stabbing the III.

At that moment, the bushes parted and Brad saw who was in them. His heart leapt into his throat, and the world fell away. It *couldn't* be.

II

THE WHITE RABBIT & THE HOLE

The white rabbit was about a foot shorter than Brad. This fact meant nothing; any rabbit that big *wasn't* a rabbit Brad wanted to cross in the night. Even with only the moonlight as a source of illumination, the rabbit's white fur appeared matted and dirty. Its vest hung off bony shoulders and its red eyes gleamed at Brad.

"That's mine," it said. Its tongue and huge front teeth caused the S sound to slightly whistle.

Brad tried to speak, tried to move, but couldn't.

"I said, 'That's *mine*,'" the rabbit repeated.

Brad blinked and looked at the pocket watch in his hand, which he had forgotten about in his surprise. He grasped it with white knuckles, his hand trembling from the force.

"I'll take that now," the rabbit said and stepped forward.

Brad dropped the pocket watch and stepped back. The rabbit's nose twitched, its whiskers bobbing up and down catching moonbeams, and scooped the watch off the ground.

"Thankee-sai," it said. "Sorry to run but I'm late."

Then the rabbit turned and hopped toward Miranda's backyard.

"Can't keep Alice waiting," it said and disappeared behind the house, into the backyard.

Alice.

Again, Brad saw Miranda, this time laughing. She laughed hard and sometimes followed it with a squeal. His heart rammed. He knew that...*thing* was talking about Miranda. Despite everything in him warning not to, he followed the White Rabbit.

The yard was small, more of a patch, really, and bordered by thin trees and shrubs. A glance at the house showed the back door open, the inside dark. Brad felt the urge to go in and check things out but knew Miranda wouldn't be in there.

The shrubs on the far side of the yard rattled with movement and took Brad out of his thoughts. The White Rabbit had probably gone through them. Crossing the yard and parting the bushes, Brad just caught the rabbit disappearing down a hole.

Of course there'd be a hole. Wasn't that how the story went? Surely there'd be a disappearing cat, a queen with a decapitation fetish, and all sorts of weird and wonderful things at the bottom of the hole. Except, something told Brad that maybe *wonderful* wasn't the right word.

He approached the hole with caution, just in case this was some sort of a trap. The rabbit couldn't be real, had to have been a massive hallucination caused by exhaustion. He told himself he should go home and call the doctor in the morning. Maybe get a prescription for something. Shit, even a phone call to Tommy would help. Tommy was great at listening and gave well-thought-out advice.

You tell the doctor about going to your friend's house at three in the morning and chasing giant white rabbits, and he'll lock you up, said the voice Brad found he disliked. *Even Tommy wouldn't know what to make of it.* Mad *is what it is. Simply mad.*

Brad looked into the hole. Black. He took a rock from the ground and dropped it in. It thumped, thunked, and otherwise bounced against the hole's walls several times, each time its sound came back fainter until it finally vanished.

Miranda's down there somewhere, he thought, heart ramming and stomach tight. *And she needs help.*

Does she really, *though?* asked the voice.

Ignoring the warnings in his head (and also ignoring the glee in the crazed voice) Brad sat on the edge of the hole, took a deep breath, and dropped in.

In the freefall state, Brad wanted to scream but couldn't find his voice. The sensation was like that moment before one fell into a deep sleep, where consciousness grasped hold with all its might but was losing, aware of nothing and everything at once while hanging in blackness.

Soon, though, he began to faintly make out the surrounding walls of the hole.

I'm going to die, he thought.

You'll be fine, the voice said.

The walls began to form around him. Stones and roots hung from the dirt. He passed through a ring that went around the circumference of the hole's walls, and then another. He counted seven more, totaling nine, before the light at the bottom of the hole made the darkness seem like a thing of the past.

For the first time, Brad saw the bottom of the hole. It was red.

III
THE SOFTLY SHARP LANDING & A JOURNEY BEGUN

R oses, Brad thought the moment before he landed in them. The roses cushioned the fall but their thorns weren't so kind. Scrambling to get out of the flowers, Brad cut the back of his hand near his thumb. Crimson blood fell on a red rose. The blood seeped into the petal and the rose grew black, trembled, and closed. A moment later, it opened revealing thorny teeth and lunged at Brad. He moved away just in time and struggled to escape the roses, which led him down a hill to a road made of old, crumbling cobblestones. Or bricks. Yellow bricks.

If I find myself wearing ruby slippers I'm going to let those roses eat me.

His sneakers remained though. Brad looked back and saw several more hungry roses had formed where his blood had dropped. They hissed and snapped and would no doubt tear themselves from the ground if they could, to get at him.

He realized there was a blue sky above him instead of an underground stone ceiling. The hole he fell out of wasn't there. He appeared to have dropped out of thin air.

Brad forced himself to ignore the impossibility of everything that was going on. Time was short and he needed to find

(alice)

Miranda. He looked down the yellow brick road, then up. Which way had the rabbit gone? Ahead of him the road split: the yellow brick road went to the right; a dirt road went to the left, and a sign rose from the ground at the Y. He figured that was a good place to start.

At the fork in the road the sign read—

ALBUQUERQUE
OZ→
←WONDERLAND

and below that, someone had added—

BEWARE THE JABBERWOCK!

In the past, choosing which way to travel may have been a long process. He could almost hear Karen laughing at his indecisiveness on such things as what to have for dinner or where to go for fun or on many other things. He wasn't much better now that they were separated. Miranda had pointed out on several occasions that he didn't seem to know what he wanted. She'd said that just recently as they sat on her porch. He sipped his chai tea as she took a drag from her cigarette.

Brad's face flushed. "Karen says that."

"Maybe she's right," Miranda said.

"Well…maybe for the small things. But I think I have the big things somewhat figured out."

He looked at her. He wanted to hold her, kiss her. He wondered what it would feel like. Would she love the same way she laughed, with everything she had? Had Karen ever loved him like that, even at the beginning as they both learned about passion? He thought not.

Brad blinked the memories away and focused again on the sign in front of him.

"What's up, Doc?" Brad mumbled, and took the road on the left. He heard dogs howling from the yellow brick road.

Passing the sign, he realized how calmly he was taking all this. He'd been worried about hallucinating a giant white rabbit just moments ago, and here he was in an entirely different world and feeling only mildly nervous.

No, that wasn't true. He was terrified. His heart rammed, his scrotum was like a walnut shell, and the hairs on the back of his neck stood on end. But what could he do about it? Miranda was in trouble.

Besides, for this to be a hallucination would mean he was truly insane, and one couldn't know he was insane. The other alternative was that he was dreaming, and Brad was almost certain he wasn't.

Stop dwelling on things, said a voice that sounded like Tommy. *Just go with it. It is what it is.*

And with that, he followed the dirt road toward a forest.

IV

THE DARK FOREST & TWO SETS OF TWINS

Not far into the forest, the treetop canopy almost completely shut out the sunlight bringing a premature dusk. Random columns of ethereal sunlight seeped through cracks in the overgrown canopy, providing just enough light to see. Before entering the forest, Brad checked his watch and stopped. It was running backwards. The position of the sun and a feeling in his gut placed him at mid-morning.

After what felt like several minutes of walking through the forest, the dirt path narrowing as he progressed, Brad wondered if perhaps he'd made a mistake. Woodland creatures made noises from the forest around him: birds from the trees, insects buzzing and creaking everywhere, and critters scurrying just out of sight. However, he saw no sign of the White Rabbit.

Until he came across a small mound of dark brown pellets, larger than normal rabbit shit. It *had* come this way.

You can be so *obtuse sometimes*, the voice said.

"Fuck off," Brad murmured and continued walking.

He hoped Miranda had also come this way and wasn't hurt. They'd known each other for two years now and had become quite good friends despite all the problems they'd been having simultaneously in their lives. It was odd because Brad wasn't a person who made friends easily, but like Tommy two years before her and Jason two years before that (it was actually Jason who introduced him to Tommy) there'd been something about Miranda. Not that he'd opened up right away, but much sooner than he would have normally. She opened up a little slower, but that was fine. She had obviously been fucked-over a time or two and was more cautious than he was. At least in this case. Somehow, the end of his marriage and the end of Miranda's relationship hadn't gotten in the way.

Their friendship had begun by accident with a chance encounter at a used bookstore where they'd both been about to grab a copy of Harlan Ellison's book *Strange Wine*. He'd let her take it, but they'd talked about Ellison for a while, about how difficult it was to find his books on the secondhand market (they both believed it was because no one wanted to part with them) and moved on to Stephen King and other writers in the bookstore's café, sipping tea with honey. Miranda loved Lewis Carroll in general, the *Alice* stories specifically.

They'd separately left the bookstore not long afterward. Brad had felt fairly happy by the encounter but also a little sad; it wasn't often that he met someone with whom he shared so many interests.

They happened to run into each other at the same bookstore a week later. He'd smiled and nodded to her but didn't feel confident enough to approach her and start up another conversation, especially after the argument he'd had with Karen that had made him seek the bookstore's refuge. Besides, he wouldn't know how to begin a conversation.

"Did your copy of *Strange Wine* come in?" she asked as he sat reading a story from a Charles Beaumont paperback.

He looked up at her and instantly remembered her smile: a sly grin that hinted at mischief under the surface. Her auburn hair was tied back tight, and she looked at him with uncompromising blue eyes. He smiled and lifted the Ellison book from the side of the chair.

She sat in the chair at the next endcap and they began talking again. Somehow, he mentioned he was at the bookstore to hide from his wife. She laughed and admitted she needed a break from the boyfriend. They left the used bookstore with each other's e-mail addresses and phone numbers. How this happened, Brad didn't know, nor did he question it.

She e-mailed him first, asking if he'd ever read H.P. Lovecraft. He replied that he owned a collection of Lovecraft's work but hadn't read it yet. She asked how he could love fantastic literature—even write it—but not have read Lovecraft? They e-mailed back-and-forth from there, and then, for the hell of it, he asked if she wanted to see a movie. She'd accepted.

From there, friendship had blossomed. Only, it'd become more than friendship for Brad almost from the start, hadn't it? The crush that had developed by the end of their first encounter had grown until it became almost unbearable. Of course, they'd both had significant others. And even now, with him a few months separated and her recently out of her relationship, Miranda wanted nothing more than friendship.

Brad accepted that, but there was still hope, wasn't there? Never say never. Even Miranda wouldn't say never to him. She said, "Not right now."

With his mind on her, he almost missed the pinwheel lying on the ground.

He stopped, looking down at the multicolored, plastic pinwheel. He was about to bend and pick it up when something crashed from the shrubbery to his right.

Startled, Brad jumped back.

A fat man with white britches around his ankles stumbled out, screaming, "Mine! It's mine! Don't you *touch* it!"

Brad couldn't speak. He looked away but not before his eyes had captured a still of this rotund man. Stringy, orange hair under a small cap, a striped shirt clinging to his flabby body, white britches around his ankles that dragged suspenders, and black and white shoes kicking up dust. A dark patch of pubic hair hid under his belly with his penis inflated toward his belly button.

The man scooped the pinwheel up, grabbing his pants at the same time.

"Dee," came a voice from the bushes. "I thought you wanted it. Why bother me when I was reading?"

"He was going to take the twirly-whirl, though," Dee said, glaring at Brad. "You're a thief. A *Bad Man*."

The bushes rattled and another rotund man that looked exactly like Dee stumbled out, pulling up his pants and snapping his suspenders back in place. He glanced at Brad and then glared at the one called Dee. He waddled to his twin, hauled back and smacked him, leaving a red handprint on the shocked and hurt face.

"You don't interrupt me for *that* and then run away!" he screamed. He spun and looked at Brad, who assumed this one's name was Dum.

"Do you fuck?" Dum asked.

"No," Brad said, without thinking.

"Liar!" the fat man screamed. "I can smell virginity a mile away and *you*, sir, are no virgin."

"I meant—"

"You don't do your own *kind*," Dum said in a far more rational voice, nodding. "Okay. I can understand *that*. I don't usually either, however, my brother here, Dee's his name, is socially *inept*. He meets a beautiful woman—or an ugly woman for that matter—and gets *flustered*. Like that *woman* we saw earlier."

The one named Dee sighed and looked off into the distance. He said,

"She with red hair,
oh, I can't compare.
Water for eyes
a mouth that never lies.
Her voice is happiness to my ears.
My heart, how it hammers,
my tongue, oh it stammers,
and she reminds me of my fears."

"Yes," Dum sighed. "That's Alice."

Brad's own heart hammered. "When did you see her?"

The twins looked at each other, then looked at Brad and shrugged.

"Sometime before the *Rabbit* rushed by," said Dum.

"That hairy, horny motherfucker," Dee said, looking along the path. Then,

"He turns my blood to acid.
Though his cock is right flaccid,
I know it will become rock
to give Alice a good—"

Dum smacked his brother in the back of his head, knocking off his cap. "Shut *up* already."

Dee turned and kicked his brother in the shin.

"You *fucker!*" Dum shouted and punched his brother in the nose. Blood splattered the ground, and soon the wrestling brothers were also on the ground.

You have found her, the voice said. *Now go and get her.*

As Brad backed away, the hitting, kicking, and biting became pinching, caressing, and kissing. He turned away and walked quickly up the path, trying to ignore the sounds of the grunting and moaning from the strange duo behind him.

He hadn't gone far when Brad came across a bouncing crow in the middle of the path. The crow bounced because someone had left a trail of breadcrumbs. It hopped, scooped up a piece of bread and gobbled it down. This happened for a few moments before it stopped and looked at Brad. The crow cawed, hissed, and flew, disappearing amid the webwork of branches and leaves that formed the forest ceiling. Brad shrugged and continued along the path. The breadcrumbs continued for a few more paces and then stopped. He stopped as well.

What about Miranda? the voice asked.

Brad ignored the voice and listened. He faintly heard sobbing under the normal forest sounds. Not far away, either. He listened for several moments. The sobbing belonged to a child and came from the right of the path.

"Hello?" Brad said, keeping his voice soft. "Is anyone there?"

The sobbing stopped. Was that a *sshh* he heard? After a moment, he said, "I won't hurt you." Then he added, "I'm looking for my friend."

He thought he heard movement in the foliage and shrubbery but couldn't be certain. After another few moments, he shrugged and continued up the path.

"Wait!" a child shouted.

Brad turned and a boy came from the woods. He couldn't have been more than eight or nine. His light blond hair caught a ray of sunlight, giving him a halo. Half a beat barely passed when a girl around the same age followed the boy onto the path. She also had blonde hair. Another set of twins? Did everything come in twos around here?

The boy looked at Brad, his fearful eyes red and puffy from crying. The girl also looked scared, though the suspicion that creased her brow and shot from her eyes made her appear less helpless.

"Are you gonna kill us?" the boy asked.

"Oh, yeah," the girl said. "I'm sure he'd tell us."

"I won't hurt you," Brad said. "I'm a little lost myself."

"You said you were looking for a friend," the girl said, crossing her arms over her pink dress.

"I am," Brad said. "A woman."

"The one in the candy house?" the boy asked, voice trembling, and stepped back.

"Candy house?" Brad asked. "No."

"Good," the girl said. "'Cause she's dead. We cooked her. She was gonna cook us but we cooked her first."

"Are you looking for the other lady?" the boy asked. "The pretty one with red hair?"

Brad's heart leapt, and he tried to remain calm. "Yes."

"We saw her," the girl said. "She came running by here a while ago. Ding-dong here almost gave us away, like he did to you."

"I'm *sorry*," the boy said.

"Where did she go?" Brad asked.

"Your girlfriend?" There was taunting in the girl's voice.

I wish, Brad thought. "My *friend*," he said

"That way," the boy said, pointing in the direction Brad had been going. "She was very pretty."

"I know," Brad said before he could stop himself. Then he looked at the children. He saw now that they were dirty. Their clothes—the girl's pink dress and ribbons and the boy's corduroys and shirt—were tattered and smeared with mud, grass, and something that could be chocolate syrup...or blood. "Do you two want to go with me?"

"Yes!" the boy said as the girl said, "No!"

They looked at each other, the boy's face a mask of sorrow, the girl's one of frustration.

"Look," Brad said. "If you want to follow behind me, just to feel safe, fine. I'm looking for my friend. That's it. I just didn't want you two to be stuck in the woods alone."

"There's lotsa creatures out here," the boy said. "I heard 'em all night."

"It's up to you," Brad said. "By the way, I'm Brad."

"I'm Hansen," the boy said and his sister smacked his arm. "Ow!"

"Daddy said to never tell a stranger your name," the girl said.

"Daddy was s'pose to kill us!" Hansen shouted. "He listened to that..."

"But he didn't kill us," the girl said.

"But if we stay in the woods we *will* die! Don't you see that? What if another of those giant rabbits come along only tries to eat us this time?"

The girl didn't like it but didn't have many other options.

She's shrewd, Brad thought.

"Her name's Gretchen," Hansen said.

Brad smiled. "Nice to meet you."

To his surprise, she curtsied. She wasn't happy about it but did so nonetheless.

"We're well-met," she mumbled. "We'll follow you. But don't try nothin' funny."

Brad raised his hands, palms up. "I wouldn't think of hurting you."

"That's what Daddy said," Hansen said, and the words chilled Brad.

V

THE CRASHED TEA PARTY & THE SCONES

The twins followed Brad for a short time. Soon, Hansen walked silently alongside him. Several minutes passed before Gretchen allowed herself to join them. The woods grew thicker and darker. The columns of sunlight that broke through the forest ceiling became fewer and fewer. Brad wondered what would happen once dusk came.

Also, he had the distinct impression that something was following them. Occasionally, branches creaked or snapped, falling to the ground. They were in the woods, he told himself, creatures no doubt scampered among the trees. Still, the feeling of something watching them, following them, wouldn't go away.

Mr. Paranoid, came the voice.

Brad smiled a little. That's what Miranda called him. She was always telling him to calm down, to relax, to not be so paranoid. He couldn't help it though. He tried, but nothing seemed to help. Fears and anxieties always filled his mind. The bravest thing he'd done recently was to finally separate from his wife, and even that scared him.

"Hey, look!" Hansen said.

They'd rounded a curve in the path and entered a clearing with a table in its center. Several of the chairs lay on their sides or backs, one had been smashed, its splintered ruins scattered over the forest floor. Broken china littered the torn and stained tablecloth. Crumbs and spilled tea also joined the broken china on the tablecloth. Set in the center, untouched amid the destruction, was a teapot on a tray. A rose lay nearby. Its top was yellow and became orange and finished as crimson near the stem, like a flame. It reminded Brad of Miranda.

"Looks like someone was having a tea party," Gretchen said.

She approached the table and Brad wanted to tell her to keep back. There was no reason for the apprehension though, and he kept his mouth shut. Hansen followed his sister, but the look on his face showed he felt the same as Brad did about this mess.

"That's blood," Gretchen said, pointing to a dark stain.

"How do you know?" Hansen asked, more from fear than skepticism.

"'Cause that's what the witch's blood looked like." Gretchen shivered at the memory and wandered away from the table, toward the edge of the clearing.

Even in the thick forest canopy's dimness, the dark stains on the tablecloth could only be blood.

Gretchen screamed at the edge of the clearing and pointed into the woods.

Hansen and Brad went to her. A carcass, blood glistening off its exposed ribcage, lay in a heap nearby. Flies buzzed, dipping down, rubbing their hands like evil masterminds and flying away again. Whatever it had been was a mystery. Whatever had destroyed it hadn't left enough to be identified. Brad gently pulled the children away from the horrific sight and toward the table. Somehow, despite the bloodstains and obvious signs of struggle and mayhem, even the table was better to look at than the carcass.

"Those weren't there before," Hansen said.

Brad was about to ask what hadn't been where before, when he saw a plate with three scones. A small placard stood in front of the plate that read—

Eat me.

"Should we eat them?" Hansen asked.

"They could be poisoned," Gretchen said. A sound came from her stomach and her hand went to it automatically. She looked up at Brad, her face growing red. "We haven't had much to eat since we left the witch's house."

"Eat 'em," a muffled voice said, and the three travelers jolted.

The teapot lid trembled, china clinking against china, and fell to the table. A mouse looked out of the open teapot with wide eyes.

"The scones were left for you," the mouse said and climbed out of the teapot completely. Its small suit was soaked with tea and the mouse made a small splash when it leapt down to the table. A bloody rip went down the mouse's jacket. "It would be *very* rude not to eat something someone has gone through so much trouble to leave for you."

"Who left them for us?" Gretchen asked, as though speaking to a talking, clothed mouse was an everyday occurrence. Then again, for a girl who killed a witch living in a candy house, perhaps talking to a mouse *was* an everyday occurrence.

"I don't know," said the mouse as it stretched its back. "All I know is that I heard you, then I heard it, then I heard you again, and it was gone."

Hansen looked at Brad. "My belly hurts."

Brad sighed. "Okay. I guess this is how the story's supposed to go."

"What?" Gretchen asked.

"Never mind," he said. "Have a scone."

Hansen and Gretchen each grabbed one and devoured the scones in a matter of moments. Brad studied his first. It appeared to have raisins in it. He took a bite and it tasted surprisingly good.

"What's going on?" Hansen shouted.

Gretchen screamed.

Brad turned, and they looked smaller. His stomach lurched, and tingles spread throughout his body. Then his perspective changed as everything around him grew. Only he knew his surroundings weren't growing. He was shrinking.

Why are my clothes shrinking, too? he thought. *That doesn't make sense.*

Stop thinking so much, the voice told him.

As his sightline became level with the tabletop, the mouse ran to the edge.

"Be careful for the cat," the mouse screamed. "But also beware of—"

Of what? Brad didn't know. The mouse was too high to be heard now. Also, it'd pulled itself away from the table's edge and no longer looked down at the now-small humans.

Maybe it was pulled away, the voice said, and Brad ignored it.

The tingling and sense of vertigo stopped, and Brad found he had shrunk to a very small size. The tabletop now appeared to be as high as a skyscraper, and the grass towered over them like trees. Hansen and Gretchen held each other, trembling.

"W-what happened?" Gretchen asked. For the moment her feistiness had disappeared, replaced with true childish fear.

"We shrank," Brad said.

That's what's supposed to happen, Brad was tempted to say but didn't. He only shrugged. Gretchen rolled her eyes.

"Now what do we do?" Hansen asked.

Brad looked around. A path that wouldn't have been visible to them at their real heights led in the direction where the main path should be.

"Let's start toward the path again," Brad said. "It's probably a good idea to keep moving."

They began walking and Brad heard something behind them. He stopped and turned. The mouse's jacket lay on the ground, shredded and blood-soaked.

"What is it?" Gretchen asked.

"Nothing," Brad said and turned forward again. Gretchen looked at him, not quite believing him but not challenging him, either.

VI

THE CATERPILLAR & THE STRONG WIND

Despite the continuing sensation that something was watching them (though not necessarily *stalking* them anymore, surely they were too small to be stalked at this point) or perhaps *because* of this sensation, Brad let his mind wander. Of course, it wandered to Miranda. Her sly smile. Her water blue eyes. The way she played with her auburn hair when she concentrated on something. Sometimes she'd trace a finger over her lips (a quirk Brad shared with her). He had often wondered what it would be like to touch those lips with his own. What it would be like if the first thing he saw when he woke up was Miranda. He thought about the way she walked when she was upset, leaning forward, staring at the floor, her nostrils flared, or the strut she adopted when she was in a good mood, like a character in an early Quentin Tarantino movie. Miranda.

Alice.

No, *Miranda*. She acted as though she had everything under control—and she often did—but there was also a lost-little-girl within her, a vulnerability that Brad had glimpsed on occasion. He thought that he might be one of the few people she allowed to see that vulnerability. If only they both hadn't just come out of long relationships. If only—

"What's that funny smell?" Hansen asked.

Brad realized he too, smelled something funny. A burnt smell that made his eyes water. Was it pot? He'd never smoked any but had been around it a few times.

"It's gross," Gretchen said.

They rounded a bend in the miniature path and came to a mushroom that was the size of a large bed. A caterpillar sat atop the mushroom holding a large, blue bong to its lips. It sucked in smoke, held, and let go. Then it smiled, its bloodshot, glassy eyes looking over Brad and the twins.

"Heeyyyy," the caterpillar said. "'Sup?" He took another hit, held, and let go. "You look like you're lookin' for somethin'. Or someone."

"We are," Hansen said. "What's that?"

"This?" The Caterpillar raised the bong. "This is somethin' you don't need to know about right now, lil man. But when you get a little older, you come see me and we'll smoke together."

"Is there somethin' I can do you for?"

"I'm not sure," Brad said. "I'm looking for my friend."

"The cute chick? The one with the red hair and bad attitude?"

"That's her," Brad said, feeling a smile grow.

"And when I say *bad attitude*, I don't mean she's a bitch, though I'm sure she can be, but I mean she's *bad*. She took a few hits with me. 'Twas cool. You wanna hit, m'man?"

He offered Brad the bong.

"No thanks," Brad said. "I feel like I've already taken a hit."

"But you ain't actin' like it," the Caterpillar said. "Look at you, all stiff and shit. Like you a hero or somethin'. You a hero?"

I'd like to be, Brad thought. He only shrugged.

"To each 'is own, man," the Caterpillar said and took a drag from the bong. "So, whatchoo gonna say when you find Pretty Alice?"

"Her name is Miranda," Brad said.

"Alice, Miranda, whatever. Names are just labels and labels are cages. Some people become their names and that's a drag. Some people make their names become them, and that's cool. I forgot my name and don't care to find it anytime soon, if you can diggit."

"I diggit," Brad said. He was the only person he knew who used the term *dig* and couldn't stop his smile.

"You're cool," the Caterpillar said. "Square, but cool." He took a hit, exhaled, then smiled at Brad. "But you ain't answered my question, man. Whatchoo gonna say to Alice when you find her?"

Brad opened his mouth but didn't say anything. He didn't really know what he'd say when he found her.

"Nothin'?" the Caterpillar asked. "That's a drag. There *must* be something."

Brad said,

"Over and under,
Side to side.
Take my hand
And we'll go for a ride.

"I have things you'll want to see
That no one can show you except me.
We'll laugh, we'll cry,
We'll live by and by.

"Over and under,
Side by side.
Please, take my hand,
We need this ride."

"That's deep, man," the Caterpillar said.

Brad was stunned. Where the hell had that come from?

"It's a little heavy, though, ain't it?" the Caterpillar asked.

"It's depressing," Gretchen said.

"I liked it," Hansen replied.

"Now, m'man, I can tell that's what you feel, but maybe you need to chill just a bit. Try somethin' else."

Brad opened his mouth to tell the Caterpillar there was nothing else, that he didn't know where the other rhyme had come from, but what came out was,

"Frapdazzle and flip,
Wapbantha and shnizzle.
Hand on your hip
As you dance in a drizzle.

"Flip and frapdazzle,
Loopty lees,
Gungans dancing
With Wookiees with fleas."

"Mexcellent!" the Caterpillar shouted and roared with laugher. "Keee-*rist!* That was good, m'man."

Brad found himself laughing; even the kids laughed at the nonsense.

"See?" the Caterpillar said. "You gotta chill out a bit. Ain't that what Alice tells ya?"

This hit like a mallet to the stomach. "Yeah. How do you know?"

"*Anyone* can see that you need to relax," the Caterpillar said. "You so serious. Besides, anyone cool enough to share Da Bong with me *must* tell you that if she's your friend."

Brad nodded.

"Look, man," the Caterpillar said and leaned forward. "You lookin' for somethin' bigger than you know. Don't look so hard. *Relax*. Some things happen on their own. Besides, you have to take care of the other guy first."

Bricks filled Brad's stomach. "What other guy?"

The Caterpillar smiled. "You know who. Search your feelings, m'man. You two be *real* close."

Brad's mind scrambled. Miranda had become a close friend, almost as close as Tommy or Jason was, and neither of them could be the other guy because they were married. If she'd gone back to her ex-boyfriend, well, Brad didn't know him at all, they certainly weren't close.

"Anywho," the Caterpillar said. "I think you people wanna get going. Take a bite of this mushroom."

"It's not poisonous, is it?" asked Hansen.

"Lil man," the Caterpillar said with mock hurt. "Do you really think I'd hurt you?"

"No," Hansen said, scuffing his toe in the dirt.

"Course not," the Caterpillar said.

At that moment, a howl came and wind blasted into them, scattering nearby leaves (which were large enough for them to use as shelter). The three humans stumbled from the wind's force.

"Ah, shit," the Caterpillar shouted above the roar of the wind. "Hurry up and take some 'shroom before the wind carries you awa*aaaayyyyy*—"

The Caterpillar was plucked off the mushroom by a strong gust, and it disappeared into the grass. Hansen and Gretchen were carried away as well, but Hansen grabbed a blade of grass and Gretchen grabbed him. Fighting the sudden gales, Brad made his way to the mushroom and tore off a chunk big enough for the three of them to share. He stumbled toward the children as the wind pushed at him. He broke off two pieces and held them out to Hansen and Gretchen. The children each held out one hand and took the pieces of mushroom.

The strongest gust of wind so far rushed at them, and Gretchen was taken away, followed a moment later by Hansen. Another strong gust swept Brad off his feet, and he joined the children in their airborne adventure.

Brad, like most children born in the twentieth century, had grown up with superheroes. While Batman was his favorite — after all, Batman was a human who had pushed himself to be the best at everything — Superman had one specific power Brad, and many other children of all ages, dreamed of: flight. Now Brad flew. Not far ahead of him, Hansen and Gretchen flew as well.

"Eat the mushroom!" he bellowed over the wind and followed his own advice.

He saw the children do the same. Every fiber in him tingled again. Whatever magic had worked to make him (and his clothes) shrink before, worked now to enlarge him (and, thankfully, his clothes). As he grew, he sank closer to the ground until he was too heavy for the wind to carry and he hit the ground. He saw Hansen and Gretchen also hitting the ground. None of them landed hard and what had seemed like a tornado wind was little more than a gusty breeze.

Brad stood on trembling legs. Hansen leaped to his feet and shrieked a laugh.

"That was *fun*!" he shouted and hooted.

Even Gretchen smiled until something caught her eye. Her mouth fell open and she screamed, pointing to a tree ahead of them.

The gnarled, knotty tree was one of many in the area, hunched over the grass. Shriveled, brown apples hung off the dark-leafed branches. A man hung from the tree, swaying.

Brad's mouth went dry and the children ran to him.

"Wait," Gretchen said, squinting at the hanging man. For a brief, terrible moment, Brad waited to hear that it was their father. The terror disappeared with Gretchen's chuckle. "That's a stuffy-man on the charyou tree."

It took a moment for him to realize that Gretchen meant the hanging man wasn't a man at all, but rather a scarecrow. Then the scarecrow's head lifted, and it turned its painted eyes to them.

VII
THE SCARECROW & HIS TALE

Gretchen screamed and stumbled back. The scarecrow's hands rose, palms up.

"Nonononono!" it said. "It's okay, Dorothy. Look. I'm fine."

Gretchen's face reddened. "My name's not *Dorothy*!"

The Scarecrow's painted eyes squinted, and its shoulders sagged (more so than they already sagged).

"Oh," it said. "Beg your pardon."

"Why are you hanging there insteada a post in a cornfield?" Hansen asked.

The Scarecrow sighed. Or imitated a sigh, Brad thought, for it didn't appear the scarecrow had lungs. Then a small tearing sound came from the hanging scarecrow, just before its stuffed body fell to the ground. Its head stayed in the noose a moment before tumbling out and landing near its body. The arms pushed the body up into a sitting position and then lifted the head.

"You'd think I'd learn by now," the Scarecrow said. "I've hanged myself seven times already, and it never works."

The three travelers approached the stuffy-man. "Why do you keep...?" Brad asked.

"Hanging myself? Oh, I've done more than that. I've leapt from the tallest tower in Emerald City. I found a pistol once." It pointed to a patch on the side of its head. "I've tried drowning. That was a mess."

"What about fire?" Gretchen asked. "We threw a witch into an oven. That worked pretty well."

The Scarecrow looked at the little girl. "You have a mean streak. Most definitely not Dorothy.

"The reason I've not tried fire is because—" again, the imitation sigh, "—it would work. And I might change my mind."

"Scarecrows have minds?" Gretchen asked.

"I didn't used to," the Scarecrow said. "But then I met…"

"Dorothy?" Hansen asked.

The Scarecrow nodded.

At that moment an apple fell, hitting the Scarecrow on the back of its head. It stumbled forward and another apple came down. Brad realized the apple hadn't fallen but had been thrown from the tree.

"Not again!" shouted the tree. "For the luvva god, please, not again. Take your depressing tales somewhere else."

"He's right," the Scarecrow said. "Come, let's walk. It's only a dirt road, but I finally decided my future lies beyond the yellow brick road."

And they headed back to the path Brad and the twins had flown over as the wind had carried them.

"I wasn't always like this, you know," the Scarecrow said as they walked. "Well…not depressed like this. I used to hang in the farmer's field. Sure, the crows and birds weren't scared of me, and sure I often wished I'd had brains, but things were simpler then. I wish I'd known."

"What happened?" Hansen asked.

Brad stopped a smile. Of course, one storybook character wouldn't know another, would he?

"*She* came along," the Scarecrow said. "She was only a little girl, a little older than you." It patted Gretchen's head and she lurched away from its stuffed hand. "But she was beautiful and smart and clever and…" It shook its head. "She'd be a woman now. I often think about her."

"You're crazy," Gretchen said.

"And you're rude," the Scarecrow replied. "She gave me the ability to see myself. To see that I already had the brain I'd always wanted, just as she showed one of my friends that he had a heart, and another that he had courage. She was like that. She brought out the best in everyone."

Brad nodded. Miranda brought out the best in him, too.

"She used the magic hat and the magic shoes," the Scarecrow continued. "And she saved the land. She said I helped her, and when she left I was made King. But I couldn't reign, not without her. As the years passed, I saw things in the world. Wrongs that could never be righted, and I realized that knowledge was the ultimate curse. While I had been sad hanging on that post, I didn't know what the world had to offer. It hurt me, but not as much as I'm hurting now. Not now that I've seen how difficult life is and how devastating knowledge can be. Now I know I was better off before."

"Then why not torch yourself?" Gretchen asked. Hansen smacked her arm, and she punched his. Brad separated the two.

"I don't know," the Scarecrow said. "I guess there's always hope that Dorothy will come back."

"My word," Gretchen said. "You sound like *him*." She nodded toward Brad. "He's looking for Alice—"

"Miranda," Brad interrupted.

"Whatever," Gretchen said, waving a hand as though trying to get rid of a fly. "Either way, you're both miserable. Why not just get over it already?"

"You're too young to understand," the Scarecrow said.

"And I think I'm stuck here until I find her," Brad said.

Gretchen sighed, shaking her head.

"Do you want to come with us?" Hansen asked.

"Will there be a wizard?" the Scarecrow asked.

Brad shook his head, again stopping a smile. "Not that I know of. At least, we're not looking for a wizard. I'm just trying to find my friend."

"Hmm," said the Scarecrow. "I think I saw her. I thought she was Dorothy but quickly realized she wasn't. I hid and she didn't see me."

"She was going this way?" Brad asked.

The Scarecrow nodded.

Gretchen sighed and mumbled something that sounded a lot like *pathetic*.

Brad, the twins, and the Scarecrow walked along the path. If the leaves on the branches rattled overhead, well, it was *probably* just the grumpy trees.

VIII

HANSEN'S SADNESS & THE CAT

Brad felt them being watched again. It was a sensation that wouldn't go away. He looked whenever a branch creaked or leaves rattled.

"We'll be out of the woods soon," the Scarecrow said.

But we're not out of them yet, Brad thought.

As they walked, Brad noticed another mound of big rabbit turds. They rounded a bend and the trees dwindled ahead as the path rose over a hill. The sun shone in golden embers, ready to set.

"I'm hungry," Hansen said.

"You're always hungry," said Gretchen. "That's how we got in trouble with the witch. You were hungry."

"But her house was made of *candy*," Hansen said. "And I saw *you* eat plenty, too."

"Of course I ate. I had to. Still, you're always hungry."

Brad patted Hansen's shoulder. "I'm hungry too," he said. "That scone wasn't very filling." He looked at Gretchen. "You must be hungry, too."

"No," Gretchen said, not very convincingly.

Hansen began crying. Not hard, but enough.

"Step-Mama usedta tell me I ate too much. She always said that I was gonna eat them outta house-n-home."

"I told you not to listen to her," Gretchen said, putting her arm around her brother. "She was as bad as the witch."

"But maybe that's why she wanted Daddy to kill us," Hansen said. "Because I eat too much. There wasn't enough to feed us and—"

"Don't be stupid," Gretchen said. "She wouldn't have wanted me dead because *you* eat too much."

"Maybe she wanted you dead because you gave her lip."

"Look," Brad said. "Whatever reason your stepmother wanted you…well, wanted you out of the picture, your father loved you enough not to go through with it."

"He left us in the woods," Gretchen said. "With no food and no water. Dad might not have wanted to kill us with his own hands, but we could've died." She sighed. "Of course, Dad's never been the sharpest tool in the shed."

"Remember how, as we were walking, he taught us which berries to eat?" Hansen said. "I bet he was gonna come back for us. We shoulda stayed where he left us, like I said."

"Well, we didn't," Gretchen said.

They walked in silence for a bit, the unpleasant conversation seeming to have run its course, when a voice from the trees to their left said, "I know where there's food."

Brad, the Scarecrow, Hansen, and Gretchen stopped and looked up. On a low branch near the side of the path sat a large cat. It wasn't quite large enough to be a mountain cat of any kind, but it was larger than the normal house cat. And it smiled, sharp teeth glistening. Brad shivered as the cat's yellow eyes looked over the travelers.

"Of course," the smiling cat said. "Nothing in life is free."

Hansen groaned.

"How much does this food cost?" Brad asked. "And what is it?"

"It's meat," the cat said. "Good, fresh meat. And the price is actually quite cheap: tell me a story."

"A story?" Brad said.

"Yes," the cat replied. "Something that will amuse me and make me...*smile*."

"It doesn't look like you have a problem smiling," the Scarecrow said.

The cat arched an eyebrow. "One could say I'm good humored."

"He tells good stories," Hansen said, nodding toward Brad.

"Good," the cat said and licked a paw. "Please, don't keep me waiting."

Brad looked ahead. They were so close to the end of the woods. Also, something about the cat didn't sit well with him. The Cheshire Cat wasn't dangerous...was he?

"Maybe there's food ahead, over the hill," Brad said.

"There *is* a kingdom ahead," the Cat said. "But last I knew, there's no one there. And if people are scarce, chances are that food is equally scarce." The cat stopped licking its paw (and claw, Brad thought) and looked at Brad with piercing eyes. "Why don't you just tell me a story?"

Because I don't know a goddamn story, Brad thought. But that wasn't true, was it? He did know stories, plenty of them. He wrote, after all. But sometimes starting one was the hard part.

Why worry about it? the voice asked. You're the one in control if they're listening.

The voice, as annoying (and somewhat unsettling) as it was, was right. It seemed that all he had to do was open his mouth and,

"*As the sunset dropped its golden rays*

I found her through the haze
That had been floating round my head
And my heart stopped, I thought I was dead.
Then the Wabwackle winked in.
He held a cane and said, 'I'm Slinkton.'
Then he lifted his lid,
said, 'How'd'yado, kid?'
Then over his head a lightbulb blinked on.

"*He took my hand and took hers, too,*
And jumped around like an ape in a zoo.
We danced and we sang.
She shook her thang.
Then Slinkton of the Wabwackles
Put me in shackles
And a club on my head he did bang."

"Ouch," the Cat said. "Not the best story I've ever heard but it's entertaining enough. Please continue."

Brad wasn't sure he could continue, yet,

"*I was unconscious for an unknown time.*
With a taste in my mouth as tart as lime,
I awoke with pain in my head.
I was a little surprised I wasn't dead.
But then I stood real quick
And started feeling sick
When I realized he'd taken her and fled."

"Oh, boy," said the Cat. "Violence and kidnapping. This is getting good. What's the woman's name?"

"Alice," Gretchen said.

"Ah, I see," the Cat said. "Please, go on."

"Slinkton had taken her up into a tower
With a door locked so tight it would take lots of power
To break it down, to get myself in,
When I got an idea and felt myself grin.
See, the tower was surrounded by billions of roses.
I bent and picked one of the closest
And the lock I put the stem within.

"The stem I wiggled and jiggled until the lock clicked.
My finger one of the thorns had pricked,
But other thorns had helped a great deal
For they had picked the lock, which was almost unreal.
But question it I did not,
Just opened the door (whose wood had begun to rot)
And in the dark, up the stairs my way I did feel."

"Using a thorny stem to pick a lock?" the Cat asked. "Well, this is obviously a fantasy tale. Very interesting. I also like the dark part." He paused and his smile somehow grew wider. "You never know what lies await in the dark." Another pause before, "Please, continue."

Speaking of the dark, the dusk grew thicker. Brad glanced toward the hill and the darkening sky. The trees' shadows had grown.

The cat's keeping us here for some reason, he thought. *And it can't be good.*

Stop worrying, the voice said. *And finish the damn story.*

Brad gulped and,

"The stone walls of the tower were moldy
But in the dark I walked rather boldly
Ignoring the sounds of things scuttling 'round
And making sure as I went my feet always touched ground.

Then, at last, I saw a light very dim,
Coming from around another door's trim.
I got to the door, listened, and heard a sound.

"Was it crying? I couldn't be sure.
I'd kill the bastard if he'd hurt her.
I didn't bother with doorknobs, just crashed my way through,
And what I saw then made me sick as the flu,
For crying wasn't what had reached my ears.
The smiles on their faces made my eyes fill with tears.
They were together and there wasn't a thing I could do."

"How bad," the Cat said. "So sad."

"So from the tower I fled and never looked back.
It'd been over for me before Slinkton did whack
Me with his club upside my head.
As I walked, I wished I were dead.
And clouds came then, and it began to rain,
Water driving down with the power of a train.
With a crash of thunder, I awoke, and found myself in bed."

"A *dream?*" the Cat asked.
"Whatta gip," Gretchen said.
"The whole thing seemed forced," said the Scarecrow. "The meters didn't really work and it felt awkward. Perhaps a modification of the Shakespearean sonnet. Cut in half, you'd still get the seven lines, which you tried to keep, but then you'd have a better flowing piece."

"It was a valiant effort," the Cat said. "And you will be duly rewarded." It stood and stretched, shivers running over the course of its body from the tippity-top of its head to the tippity-tip of its tail. "Follow me."

The cat jumped down from the tree, landing without much sound considering the height it had dropped, and began slinking its way into the woods.

Brad didn't like the idea of going deeper into the woods. Not with their end so near and with the feeling they were being stalked. Although, the feeling *had* somewhat abated.

"Are we going or not?" Gretchen asked.

"He said there's food," Hansen said, rubbing his belly. "Meat."

Brad looked at the Scarecrow, who shrugged. "Don't look at me. I don't eat meat." A pause. "For that matter, I don't eat anything."

"Friends," the Cat called. "Are you coming?"

The children looked up at Brad. Hansen's eyes were round, pleading, and even under her attitude Gretchen's eyes held the hope that he'd say yes.

Brad sighed. "Okay."

And despite the feeling that this would be a terrible decision, the four followed the cat as it wove through the trees, deeper into the darkening woods and the waiting trap.

IX

THE TRAP & THE AWFUL TASK

In the forest's growing dimness, they had a hard time keeping track of the cat and would have become lost if it hadn't kept turning toward them with its glowing yellow eyes. Brad's anxiety grew the deeper into the woods they went.

"*Over and under / Side to side,*" Hansen mumbled, almost inaudibly. "*Take my hand / And we'll go for a ride.*" He repeated the four lines like a mantra.

Brad smiled. He didn't know why, exactly, it wasn't as though he'd been carrying that rhyme (or any of the others he'd said this day) with him for a lengthy time, but it was kind of nice to have someone who so obviously looked up to him.

I'm nobody's role model, he thought. It was something he'd said to Miranda not long ago.

Don't be so sure, had been her reply.

Though it had become almost too dark to see, Brad could just make out a small clearing. He couldn't see the Cheshire Cat, though.

"Where'd the kitty go?" Gretchen asked.

They looked around, silent. Not even nocturnal woodland creatures stirred. The occasional breeze rattled leaves, but no other sound came.

"I have a bad feeling about this," Hansen whined.

"Don't be stupid," Gretchen said. "You never have a good feeling about—"

At that moment a hissing growl rose from nothing and Hansen flew back, screaming. Four rips opened his shirt and flesh. Blood spurted and Hansen cried.

"*Help!*" he screamed.

His throat burst open, the white flesh parting. Hansen's hands seemed to be wrestling with the air immediately in front of him. It was then that Brad realized what was going on.

He ran over, ignoring Gretchen's screams and the Scarecrow's shouts, and kicked at the air above Hansen. His foot made contact with something soft but heavy.

Meeroow!

Several feet away, yellow eyes and a bloody grin floated in the air.

Hansen didn't move, didn't cry. His glazed eyes stared at the forest's dark canopy but didn't see it.

The nearly invisible cat laughed. A hiss followed and the glowing yellow eyes and dripping red teeth rose as the Cat pounced at Brad.

He leapt to the left, the Cat's claw ripping through his jacket and shirt and cutting his side. He winced at the stinging heat. Blood rolled down his side but he knew the cut wasn't deep. This time.

The Scarecrow yelled out and Brad saw straw flying from a new opening in its stomach.

"Gretchen!" Brad yelled.

She knelt beside her brother, holding him. His blood seeped into her already dirty clothes and she wept. Brad caught sight of the glowing eyes heading for her. He rushed toward the girl and kicked out, again connecting with the invisible cat. It kicked up fallen leaves and pine needles as it slid across the forest floor.

The eyes soon rose again, though, and the cat let out another hiss.

Brad swept Gretchen off the ground. She fought him, screaming and reaching for Hansen

(he ain't hearing nothing no more)

(shut up)

but he held tight.

"Let's get outta here!" Brad yelled.

The Scarecrow grunted its agreement, trying to keep straw in its new opening.

"*Put me down!*" Gretchen screamed.

As Brad ran, he heard the Cat giving chase. He was certain that it would leave the Scarecrow alone for now (as long as the Scarecrow kept running and didn't try to stop it—it wanted meat, after all) but he was also sure that the enraged cat would tear the Scarecrow apart for the fun of it, after it had caught its real prey. Brad just hoped that it wouldn't catch its real prey.

Leaves rattled above him and he sensed something falling from the trees. He leapt to the right, dropping Gretchen. The smiling Cheshire Cat, in full view, landed on the ground. It looked at Brad and faded into the darkness, leaving only its toothy smile.

"I've got a rhyme for you," the Cat said. "*Through the teeth / Over the gums / Look out tummy / Here it comes.*"

Twigs and leaves exploded in a dusty plume (seemingly by air alone) and Brad took the chance that the Cat was headed for him. He hoped it would try to take him out before Gretchen simply because, now that the surprise was over, he posed more of a threat than she did. He swept his arms out and caught something thick and furry, though invisible.

The Cat growled and hissed. Invisible claws tore through Brad's sleeves and arms. Clenching his teeth, he tried to ignore the pain and quickly found the spot where the cat's tail met its back. He grasped the fluffy tail and held it away from his torso. The Cat slashed at him, at one point tearing through his leg, just above the knee. Brad held the tail with both hands, fighting the large, heavy cat's struggling and wriggling, and swung. Moss that had grown up the side of the tree crumbled off from the impact and there was a thud-snap. Brad swung again for good measure and there was another thud and more crumbling moss. The Cheshire Cat struggled no more.

He let go of the tail and it hit the ground. The Cat faded back in, its eyes rolled up, its tongue lolled out, and its head at a strange angle.

The adrenaline that had carried him this far disappeared like the cat had, and Brad's legs trembled, threatening to give out. To remain standing, he held onto the tree he'd smashed the Cat against. Behind him, Gretchen sobbed. The Scarecrow stood silent. Several moments passed that way.

"The path is right up ahead," the Scarecrow said softly, breaking the silence. "Maybe we should get back on it before it grows darker."

"Yeah," Brad said. He didn't feel much stronger but let go of the tree nonetheless.

Gretchen was on her knees, looking down with slumped shoulders that shook with each sob she made. He held a hand out to her.

"Come on, honey," Brad said, voice soft. "The Scarecrow's right."

"What about Hansen?"

Brad gulped. She *had* to know; she'd held him. Maybe it was shock. "I'm sorry. He's—"

"I know he's dead!" she shouted. "I mean, we can't just leave him out here like this. We need to bury him."

Brad looked at the Scarecrow, who shrugged. "Will you do it?" Brad asked.

"I think *you* should," Gretchen said. "You brought us out here." And then, in a softer, almost inaudible voice: "And he liked you a lot."

Brad looked again at the Scarecrow who wouldn't make eye contact with him. He sighed. "Okay."

"We'll be on the path," the Scarecrow said. "Waiting."

Brad nodded.

Gretchen rose, took the Scarecrow's hand, and Brad watched them walk toward the path in the deepening dark. Then he turned, hoping he could remember where the Cheshire Cat (or this version of it) had sprung its trap, and began walking in the direction from which they'd run.

How'd I get myself into this? Brad wondered as he walked through the dark woods. He hoped he was heading in the right direction. He also hoped he wouldn't get lost.

Haven't you felt lost for a while now? the voice asked.

He wanted to ignore the annoying voice but found it difficult. He *had* felt lost for a long time, which was one of the reasons why he liked being with Miranda so much. It felt right to be with her. They never seemed to run out of things to talk about. What silences they shared were comfortable; just hanging out was good enough.

Then why won't she let you guys go to the next level?

Because...

Miranda was one of the first people he'd trusted in a while. The only other friend he trusted as much was Tommy, but they didn't get to see each other often since Tommy had moved up to New Hampshire, had married Leigh, and had had a son. As a matter of fact, Brad had taken Miranda up to visit Tommy, Leigh, and their newborn son Ryan. Brad had been meaning to visit his best friend's new son anyway and thought it'd be a good chance to see what Tommy thought about Miranda. His friend Jason was another person he trusted a lot, but didn't get to see nearly as often as he would've liked.

Tommy and Miranda both came from the same town and had seemed to hit it off well enough. They talked about a large range of things and all went out to dinner, followed by a trip to a bookstore. It'd been good fun. The next day, Brad had called Tommy to see what he thought of Miranda.

"She's cool," Tommy had said.

"Did you see anything?" Brad had asked. "Am I crazy or was there chemistry between us?"

"Well…" Tommy said. One of the things Brad loved about his best friend was his measured responses. "I'm not really sure. I mean, there's definitely comfort between the two of you, but I don't know that there's anything more than that."

Brad sensed hesitancy in Tommy's words. He knew Tommy well enough to know this was partly because he hadn't seen much of Brad and Miranda together, but also because he hadn't seen anything more than friendship between them either, and didn't want to hurt his best friend. Brad was sure that given more time with the two of them, Tommy would be able to see more. His and Miranda's friendship was great, but Brad *knew* they could be great together as lovers, too. If only there was some way to show her…

The woods opened and Brad found himself in the small clearing again. It was almost too dark to tell if this was the place where the cat had turned on them. The sounds of slurping and chewing came from the dark, and as Brad's eyes grew used to the nuances of the area, he realized that the woodland creatures he'd not heard before were not only audible now, but were munching on Hansen's corpse.

"Get!" he said. "Shoo! Scat!"

Several raccoons scuttled into the woods. Even in the dark, Brad could tell there wasn't much left of the little boy. He lifted what was left and carried him to an area near the edge of the clearing. He put Hansen's body down and dug into the ground with his bare hands. Cold soil packed under his fingernails and he scraped his knuckles on rocks several times. He wouldn't be able to dig six feet down and didn't try. There were enough leaves, branches, and rocks to help cover the body. Besides, if one were to believe that a body could be desecrated, Hansen's half-eaten body would surely have reached that point by now.

Brad made a shallow grave, placed Hansen's body gently into it, then covered it with soil. He then added leaves, branches, and rocks. An unknown amount of time passed as he worked. Time seemed bendable in this world, and like any task that one didn't want to do, this task seemed to last forever.

Finally, Brad stood, his knees crying out as they straightened, and his lower back ached. He stretched, trying to get his bearings. Once he remembered where he'd come from, he went in that direction.

He hoped Miranda was safe, wherever she was. She was sharp and might have found a way out of this nightmare. Probably had. He, on the other hand, felt his heartbeat quicken. Any chance that this was a dream was gone. How could he get out? He didn't know. Finding Miranda had to be the way it went.

He heard the muffled voices of the Scarecrow and Gretchen. Good. He was near the path and they *had* waited for him. He should've been approaching the spot where he'd killed the cat right about—

The tree with the portions of missing moss stood to his right. So the cat should have been—

No. Brad knelt to the spot where the Cheshire Cat's dead body had dropped.

Maybe it went invisible again, the voice taunted.

Brad felt around for something furry, meaty, but nothing lay on the foliage. Perhaps a creature had come and taken it away, just as some had been munching on—

Brad vomited on the spot where the cat had been. The voices of the other two stopped behind him. When he'd finished, he wiped his mouth and stood, inhaling the cool air deeply. It filled his lungs and helped push the dizziness away.

That's what it had to be. Another creature. Or several of them. He'd killed the goddamn thing, he *knew* he had.

"Umm...Brad?" the Scarecrow called.

"Yeah," Brad replied. "It's me. Sorry."

"Are you all right?"

"Yeah," he lied. "Yes." Then he met his companions on the path.

X

OUT OF THE WOODS & THE OLD PEOPLE

Though the woods had reached full night, the western horizon beyond the woods was crimson, and the sky grew darker until it became purple, then black on the farthest reaches of the eastern horizon. Brad, Gretchen, and the Scarecrow stopped on the dirt path just outside the edge of the woods. The land rose in front of them and the path went over the hill.

Gretchen turned and looked into the woods where her brother had died. Tears shimmered in her eyes. She wiped them, mouth trembling but set, unwilling to release the words or sobs that no doubt wanted to come. Brad and the Scarecrow glanced at each other, and Brad put a hand on her shoulder. It rested there only a moment before the girl seemed to remember her tough façade and pulled her shoulder away. She walked quickly up the hill and Brad and the Scarecrow followed her, not allowing Gretchen to get too far ahead.

"Dorothy most assuredly was *not* like this one," the Scarecrow mumbled. "Oh, no. She was sweet and kind, and she had a big heart and—"

"She just lost her brother," Brad said. "Cut her a break."

The Scarecrow walked silently for a moment before mumbling, "*I* wasn't the one given a heart."

Gretchen stopped at the top of the hill and gasped. A moment later, Brad and the Scarecrow joined her. Brad didn't gasp (and the Scarecrow couldn't without lungs) but he did feel tingling in his belly and a rising sensation in his heart. Excitement. The hill dropped into a valley and the path became an actual road. By the road, near another, smaller hill with a well at the top, sat a small wood house with one lit window. Much farther away, miles and miles past the small house, stood a castle.

In the setting sunlight, the castle appeared every bit a fairy tale castle. Triangular flags fluttered in the breeze. A moat ran around the castle with a drawbridge connecting one side to the other. Once this last detail set in, Brad's feet grew cold and his stomach sank. No castle, even one in a fantasy world, left its drawbridge down. Something was terribly wrong with this.

"Are we gonna just stand here all day or are we gonna go to the castle?" Gretchen asked.

Brad opened his mouth to answer but the Scarecrow said, "It's not as close as it looks. It'll take us a few hours to get there and it's getting late."

"So what?" the girl asked.

"So, maybe we should go see if the light in that house means anyone's home. We can see if they'll let us stay on their front porch."

"Waitaminute, straw man," Gretchen said, her hands on her hips and a scowl on her face. "Let me get this straight: you want to go down, knock on some stranger's door, and ask if we can shack up at their place? My brother and I were almost killed because we went to a stranger's house."

"Maybe you two can eat," the Scarecrow offered. "And I suggested resting on the porch, not inside the house."

Gretchen's sharp brown eyes shot to Brad. "What do *you* think?"

Brad found it difficult to answer. This girl would grow up to be one shrewd woman. If she grew up, that was. What was the life/death ratio for children who lived in fairy tales? With big bad wolves, wicked witches, and other assorted creatures and peril, Brad thought, realistically, the mortality rate of children in fairy tale worlds was quite high. Finally, he managed, "Well, I don't know."

"Figures," Gretchen said.

"I mean," Brad continued, "I think the Scarecrow might be right about the food, at least."

She sighed. "Fine. Let's go." She started down the hill.

Gretchen's boldness evaporated as they approached the small house. The shingles were an unpainted, weathered gray. The front porch held a rocking chair and an empty plant pot hung from a rusted chain. Light flickered in the corner window. Gretchen stared at the house, fear and hope somehow mixed on her face. Brad understood. His stomach groaned, asking to be fed, yet it also tingled with anxiety. He'd spotted another mound of rabbit turds on the side of the road, so he knew they were going in the right direction. Still, a lot could happen. He wouldn't be happy until he knew, absolutely *knew*, that Miranda was all right.

"Well?" Gretchen said, her voice barely above a whisper. She tried to fill the word with attitude but failed on that mark.

The Lil Terminator is human after all, the voice said.

Brad ignored it and climbed onto the porch. The old boards creaked under his weight. He looked at the Scarecrow, who nodded. Gretchen tried scowling, but again, her fear wouldn't quite allow her to pull it off. Brad raised a fist, about to knock on the door when it swung open and a double-barreled shotgun poked out through the crack.

"Who are ye and whatta ye want?" an old woman screeched.

Brad's mouth had gone dry the moment he realized he was looking down the deep, black caverns of shotgun barrels. He opened his mouth to answer the old woman's demands but nothing came. Behind him, still on the ground in front of the porch, Gretchen sighed.

"We've been traveling for a while," she said in a sweet voice Brad had never heard from the little girl. "We wondered if you would be so kind as to spare us some food and maybe allow us to spend the night on your porch."

The old woman with the shotgun turned her gray eyes to Gretchen. She studied the Scarecrow and then looked over Brad again. Suspicion filled her eyes. The shotgun lowered a few inches, not quite out of harm's way, but rather than blowing Brad's face off it might ventilate his stomach instead. The woman sniffed the air and then indicated the dark stains on Brad's jacket and Gretchen's dress.

"Blood," the old woman said. "Whose blood? Where from?"

"My brother's," Gretchen said. The harshness that had been so prevalent in her voice and the sweet act she had put on for the old woman was now gone. It was the voice of a scared little girl, just as it should be. "He was killed a little while ago." Tears shimmered in her eyes.

Gretchen's words reached the woman and she lowered her shotgun all the way. "A brother ye say?"

Gretchen nodded.

"Dead? *Killed?*"

Another nod.

"Oh, my," the old woman said and looked to the porch. "Very well. Ye may come in. All of ye. But I haven't enough water fer ye all. Ye'll have to fetch a pail at the top o' the hill."

Gretchen nodded. "We can do that."

The old woman looked at them all again. This time the suspicion in her eyes had been replaced by a faint sadness, possibly from a long ago incident revisited, but who knew for sure?

"Very well," she said. "Come in, come in."

The house was every bit as small on the inside as it looked on the outside. The furnishings had seen many, many moons. Trinkets and papers collected over the years, over the decades, littered almost every surface. The house smelled of old herbs and the ghost of pipe smoke past. The front room had a stone fireplace, a sofa, and a chair seating an old man. The old man's face was slack, his mouth hung open and drool glistened in the fire's orange light. The old woman led her guests past the old man and into the small kitchen. Unlike the cluttered front room, the kitchen was tidy. The pots and utensils hanging from hooks were old and must have cooked thousands of meals, but they were clean. The table was small, used to having only two people to seat, but would be perfect for them.

"The well be up yonder, on top o' the hill," the old woman said, pointing out a window near the back door. "I suggest *he* go and fetch the water." She nodded to the Scarecrow.

"I can do it," Gretchen said.

"Nope," the old woman said. "Nope-nope. Too dangerous. Ain't gonna let it. Either the straw man goes or the man goes. Simple as that."

"I'll go," the Scarecrow said. "You two can eat."

And so it went. They were given bread, cheese, and some smoked meat. When the Scarecrow returned with the pail of water, the old woman made tea. After he and Gretchen ate, a surprisingly full Brad asked if they could spend the night on her porch.

"Nay," the old woman said. "That'd be improper. Ye may stay in the parlor. If I had another room, I'd let ye chile sleep there."

In the parlor, the old man continued staring blankly into the fire. A knot popped but the old man didn't respond.

"Jack," the old woman yelled, leaning close to the old man. "Jack! We gots comp'ny." She used a handkerchief in the front pocket of Jack's shirt to wipe the drool from his chin. "Comp'ny, I say!"

Jack's dull gray eyes moved slowly up until he looked at the old woman, and he said, "Aaahhhggghh." More drool rolled down his chin.

The old woman sighed and shook her head. She sat on the sofa and took a pipe from an ashtray that rested on a small table nearby. She filled the bowl with tobacco and lit it, then puffed. The sweet-smelling smoke soon filled the room.

Brad, Gretchen, and the Scarecrow sat on the old, thin carpet.

"He's not been the same since…" The old woman sighed, looking toward the ceiling but no doubt seeing a place far beyond that, a place years—decades—in the past. "We were but chillun ourselves. We went up the hill to fetch a pail o' water. Jack fell down, broke his crown." She knocked on her own head. "I tumbled down after. Lucky for me, Jack cushioned my fall. Unlucky for 'im, his crown hit a rock. Not a big'un, mind ye, but big enough to break the ol' noggin. Ain't been right since."

"Groob," Jack mumbled.

"Ye keep yer piehole shut," said Jill (Brad suspected that was the old woman's name…what else could it possibly be?). "Ye kept me from livin' me life. I missed the Prince's ball and that…that ne'er-do-well with her glass slippers got 'im. Didja 'ear me? *Glass slippers*, mind ye. Who'd wear clogs made o' glass? Not I, oh nope. Not Jill Hill. Nope nope. But *she* gets Princey and I getsta stay wit' me feeb of a brother." She stood and pointed a thin, wrinkled, crooked finger at him. "God*damn*ye!" She stomped to the old man and slapped him. "Damn ye!"

"Yiiilll!" Jack cried out. "Yiiillll! Aaahhhhtuh!"

"Damn yer water," she said in a trembling, sad voice that was barely more than a whisper. "Damn yer water and damn ye." Then she leaned in and kissed Jack's cheek gently. "Come, ye big galoot. Time fer bed."

She pulled his wrist and Jack slowly stood. She led him out of the front room. "Ye folks keep a good night. I'll make y'all breakfast t'morrah morn."

Then Jack and Jill left the room. Brad, Gretchen, and the Scarecrow remained on the floor for several moments in silence.

"That's so sad," Gretchen said.

"Yeah," Brad agreed.

"You two should try and get some sleep," the Scarecrow said.

"He's right," Brad said. "You can take the sofa, Gretchen. I'll take Jack's chair."

The chair was old but comfortable. Soon, Gretchen snored softly from the sofa.

"You going to stay here?" Brad asked the Scarecrow, feeling his eyes growing heavy.

"Of course," the Scarecrow said. "Where else would I go?"

Brad was going to say he didn't know and ask the Scarecrow to tell him, but was asleep before he could speak.

He was too tired to dream. Even of Miranda.

XI

BREAKFAST & THE CASTLE

The next morning, Jill rose before the travelers. The aroma of cooking food filled the house and made waking up quite pleasant. Brad felt rested, a feeling that wasn't common for him of late. Gretchen smiled as she stretched on the sofa. The Scarecrow's voice came from the kitchen, talking to Jill. Even Jill sounded in better spirits than she had the previous night.

As Brad and Gretchen entered the kitchen, Jill nodded in greeting. "'Morn," she said. "Yer straw friend here is quite the fella. Does he ever have anything *happy* to say?"

"Ignorance is bliss," the Scarecrow said. "Ask Folly."

"Don't know 'er. But if she comes 'round I will." Jill nodded toward the backdoor. "Gotta outhouse back there if ye need to do yer stuff."

Brad did, and apparently, so did Gretchen. So they went into the yard. The outhouse stood before the hill with the well atop. Brad waited in the sun, breathing air devoid of any fumes from cars or factories or anything else that had tinged the air since the Industrial Revolution. Gretchen came out of the outhouse.

"All yours," she said and headed back to the house.

Brad did what he needed and also returned to the house. By now, breakfast was served and Jack had come to the table. He slowly lifted a triangle of heavily buttered toast to his open, slobbery mouth. Gretchen was already munching on eggs, toast, and bacon. Brad sat, and Jill served him a heaping plate of food. As she sat in a chair across the room, Brad asked if she were going to join them.

"Oh, I had me oats and wheat already," Jill said. "That stuff ye're eatin' goes right through me and I'd spend the morn in the shithouse."

This made Gretchen giggle around a mouthful of eggs. Soon, breakfast was over and the three decided the time had come to move on.

Jill followed them to the front door and watched as they walked down the porch steps and headed up the road toward the castle.

"Keep well," Jill called after them. "And please visit again after ye find what yer lookin' for."

They waved to her, told her they would, and carried on. Brad knew he wouldn't return to the small house where Jack and Jill had ended up. Judging from the somber look on Jill's face, she knew as well.

The Scarecrow had been correct the night before; it took a long time to reach the castle. Brad guessed it'd been about two hours, but it may have been longer. Just the size of the castle—and the road as it grew closer to the kingdom—made Brad think they were closer to it. However, both the road and the castle grew more than Brad had thought possible. This castle had to be unequaled by anything in his world.

The pink exterior almost sparkled in the sun. The triangular flags on the turrets flapped in the breeze. As they got closer, though, Brad's stomach sank. For such a vibrant looking castle there was little happening around it. The drawbridge remained open, which was odd enough, but no noise came from inside the castle walls. No signs of life except for birds—large birds—circling in the sky.

Vultures, the voice said. *And some crows. Scavengers.*

They finally approached the castle. The water in the moat barely moved, appearing glass-like. Something floated toward the drawbridge. Cloth of some kind. Torn and stained. Blood? Brad believed so. There were enough bloodstains on him and Gretchen to be able to recognize the look.

"It's awfully quiet," the Scarecrow said. "Emerald City was nothing like this. People laughing and talking and music playing and—"

"Why didn't you stay?" Gretchen asked.

"Because I knew better. I knew that underneath were rapists, wife-beaters, pedophiles, murderers, liars—"

"All right, all right," Gretchen said. "Sorry I asked."

They stopped in front of the drawbridge. The wood was worn from years and years, perhaps centuries, of traveling feet, hooves, and wheels. The castle's gaped mouth revealed an empty courtyard. Bales of scattered hay and vacant merchant stands stood waiting. That was all they could see from this side of the moat. Brad considered trying to go around the castle but abandoned the idea when he realized a mound of rabbit turds sat at the far corner of the drawbridge, right near the hinge connecting it to the castle. Could Miranda be here? Why not?

"I don't like it," Gretchen said.

"It doesn't seem like a good idea to enter this place," the Scarecrow said.

"We have to," Brad said. His cold feet, his rapid heartbeat, and his fluttery stomach argued differently. He thought of Miranda's smile (one that actually wasn't all that different from the Cheshire Cat's). "We have to," he reiterated.

He stepped onto the drawbridge and walked toward the opening. A moment later, he heard Gretchen and the Scarecrow following.

The courtyard was every bit as lifeless, once they were inside, as it had appeared from outside. Merchant stands resided throughout the courtyard before the wall of the castle proper. Bales of hay and abandoned carts and carriages also dotted the area. Though there were no signs of life, there were many humans and animals. Dead. Horses still attached to their carts and carriages lay dead, flies buzzing over the torn flesh with dried, brown blood. People lay scattered, throats torn open, limbs torn off, portions eaten. Eaten. The Cheshire Cat? Could it have been? What the hell had happened in Wonderland?

"I *knew* we shouldn't have come in," Gretchen said, voice trembling. "I *knew* it."

Brad gulped down bile. He looked at the Scarecrow, whose painted eyes looked from one nightmare to another. His body language was stilted, shocked. Brad looked around. That sensation of being watched had returned. That goddamn cat *hadn't* been dead. How could it have survived? The cracking he'd heard when he'd smashed it into the tree *had* to have killed the fucking thing.

Why does it have to be the cat? the voice asked. *In this world? It could be something else.*

True. Too true.

"We should go back," the Scarecrow said. "If we have to continue on, perhaps we can go around the castle."

"Yeah," Gretchen said. "The Scarecrow's right. We should go back."

"No," Brad said and faced the entrance to the palace proper. "No retreat, no surrender."

"But—" the Scarecrow said.

Brad turned on him and looked straight into the straw man's painted eyes. "If you want to turn back, go ahead." He looked at Gretchen. "You, too. I'm not going to make you come with me if you don't want to, but I'm not going back."

He turned his back on them and walked toward the entrance to the palace. They soon followed. He wasn't sure if he was glad they did.

XII
INSIDE THE PALACE & THE GARDEN BEYOND

More bodies lay strewn about the palace's corridors. Some truly bad shit had gone down here, and Brad didn't like it at all. But what could he do? He may have chosen to enter the castle, but he hadn't chosen to come to Wonderland or Oz or Storyland or wherever the hell he was. Sure, he'd chosen to follow the dirty, malnourished rabbit down the hole, but had it been much of a choice? It was that or sacrifice his friend. Miranda deserved better than that. He would've done the same for Tommy or Jason. Hell, he would've done the same for Karen, too. That's just what you did for someone you cared about.

Dried blood stained the walls and tattered banners. Flies buzzed. Maggot colonies festered on several bodies.

"I think I'm gonna puke," Gretchen said.

"That's fine," Brad said.

He breathed through his mouth but the scent of rotting dead still lingered.

The corridor led to the throne room. Above the thrones at the far end of the long room was a large, red heart. Only one mutilated carcass lay in this room, not far from the steps leading to the thrones. Judging by the bright colors on its torn and bloodied clothes, and the cap with bells lying nearby, the carcass had once been the court jester.

"Who's the more foolish?" Alec Guinness had asked Harrison Ford in *Star Wars*. "The fool or the fool who follows him?"

Call me a fool, Brad thought and approached the thrones.

As he walked along the maroon carpet,

(perfect for hiding blood!)

he saw a niche in the wall with an open door. A stone path led away from the door. Bright green grass and flowers grew on either side of the path before it turned out of sight. Brad went to the door, mildly aware of the other two behind him.

The open door led to a garden. The garden had more flowers, bushes, plants and decorations than Brad had ever seen. He walked along the stone path as it wound through shrubbery. He came out and found at least an acre of hilly, rocky land in front of him, belonging to the garden. Large cards with heads and hands (*the soldiers*, he remembered) lay on the ground, some cut in half with congealing blood. Dead, half-eaten flamingos, people, and other clothed creatures were scattered about. A woman who could only have been the Queen of Hearts lay without a head. Several dead hedgehogs also littered the playing field. All had been torn at, massacred. The only living thing among the dead, besides Brad and his friends, was the large, matted, skinny White Rabbit. It held its face in its paws and wept.

"Gone!" it cried. "They're gone. Ooooooooh, they're *gone!*"

Its paws dropped to its sides, and if it could make real fists, Brad believed it would have. Its arms trembled and its muscles strained through the thin, matted white fur. The White Rabbit looked to the sky.

"*Whyyy???*" it screamed.

The White Rabbit picked up a flamingo with a snapped neck, spun, and threw it. Then the Rabbit stopped, red eyes on Brad, Gretchen, and the Scarecrow. It blinked before recognition filled its eyes.

"You," the White Rabbit said. "You were outside Alice's house. I *knew* you were trouble. I just *knew* it."

It hopped over to Brad, whose heart rammed.

"What did you do?" the Rabbit yelled. "What the fuck did you do?"

It leapt high and its feet pistoned out, connecting with Brad's chest. Brad flew back, landing on the grass near the headless body of the Queen of Hearts.

"I'll kill you!" the White Rabbit yelled.

"No!" Gretchen screamed as the White Rabbit approached Brad, its buckteeth glistening and ready to tear into him.

The Rabbit turned toward Gretchen.

"He didn't do anything," she said. "We've been with him and he hasn't done anything."

"Why should I believe you?" the White Rabbit asked.

"Why should I lie?" asked Gretchen.

The Rabbit studied her, breathing fast. Finally, its shoulders slumped and it slowly hopped away from Brad.

"I'm sorry, fella," the White Rabbit said. "I just thought I'd come here, see Alice, and play some croquet. I didn't think I'd find…*this*."

Brad rose, brushing grass off him. "It's okay. I guess it's understandable."

The White Rabbit tugged on the watch chain and looked at its pocket watch.

"If only I'd been on time," it said. "But I'm always late. It's never the right time."

Brad nodded, thinking about what Miranda had said in a soft, understanding voice when he'd confessed his love for her.

Now's just not the time. They'd been in her car, sitting on a rocky beach on East Beach Road near Horseneck Beach in Westport. Miranda's Thinking Place. They sat parked on the beach, watching the midmorning sun glimmer on the Atlantic Ocean.

Then something the White Rabbit said struck Brad. The Rabbit had expected to meet Alice here? Brad's heart leapt into his throat.

"Is she here?" he asked the Rabbit. The urgency, the force in his voice made the Rabbit step back. "Is she? Goddamnit, *is she?*"

"Who?" the Rabbit asked.

"Miranda—Alice—*whatever* she's called over here. Is she here?"

"No!" the Rabbit said, frightened by the man who now stood inches away from him. "At least, I didn't see her. And I've been looking all night. I thought *you* took her."

Brad blinked. "Me?"

"Yes," said the Rabbit. "That's why I kicked you. I thought you took her because…well, this looks like something you would do."

As though standing in the garden of a pink castle talking to a large rabbit, traveling with a girl from Grimm's Tales and the Scarecrow from Oz wasn't enough, this new accusation truly made the world feel dreamlike.

"How could you say that?" Brad asked. It wasn't an accusation, but he truly wanted to know. "You don't know me."

The White Rabbit stared at Brad for several beats but never answered the question, instead saying, "We have to find Alice."

"Yes," Brad said. "We do."

The garden led into a copse. Not thick woods like they'd had to travel through the previous day, but woods nonetheless. The White Rabbit now hopped along with Gretchen, the Scarecrow, and Brad. They came to a pink stone wall with a large crack in it. Gretchen needed help getting through the crack, but they soon made it beyond the border of the Kingdom of Hearts. A short while later, they found a dirt path much like the one they'd been following before coming to the kingdom.

Through it all, Brad was sure they were being watched.

XIII

THE CAT & THE BIG BAD WOLF

N ow that we've arrived at chapter thirteen, which I believe we'd all agree to be an unlucky number, we'll part from our heroes (or as we'd say in post-modern literature, our *protagonists*) and visit with our bad guys (or *antagonists*). We won't stay with them long, mind you. With a story as ghastly and grizzly as this one is turning out to be, staying with such types would not enrich our lives any. However, what the bad guys are doing—or rather, what *these* particular bad guys are doing, for there is one other, far nastier bad guy who we will meet later—is rather important to our tale, so…

Nine lives. Thank the gods for small favors. Had the Cheshire Cat not had nine lives (well, four lives…lives could be difficult to hold onto for a kitty, even one as nasty as this particular kitty could be) he wouldn't be here now. After that rat bastard had smashed him into the tree, thereby disposing of life #6, the Cheshire Cat came back from the black. His eyes fluttered and their moisture quickly returned, removing the tiny bits of moss that had clung to them since he'd died. His back and neck ached where they'd been snapped, but he knew from experience that those pains would fade soon enough. He stood, heard the rat bastard coming back, and got off the path just soon enough to miss being found. The rat bastard had stopped, looked around, and the Cat had done everything he could not to laugh. Then the rat bastard left and headed back toward his companions. How yummy he would be. How tasty the little one would be. As tasty as her brother? Perhaps. Unfortunately, he knew the morons in this neck of the woods (shit, in *any* neck of the woods) would be eating *his* meal right now. This pissed him off, and normally he'd go and end any dinner party the little scavengers might be having. However, such was not the case that night. Coming back from death took a lot of energy and he needed to be careful; he remembered disposing lives #1 and #2 back-to-back. Ah, youth and naïveté at its finest.

He should've known the man would be as crafty as he had been. After all, look who'd asked the Cat to make this man's journey here as difficult as possible. That was how things worked sometimes, but still, with three lives remaining, the Cheshire Cat knew he couldn't take many more chances. He'd need help with the man, especially since the rat bastard had made friends. Together they'd be stronger after the death of the little boy. The sweet, tasty little boy.

Oh, the Cat cursed himself for having fucked up. It was almost inexcusable. Almost. Yes, he'd need help. It may cost him another life, but be that as it may, there was only one who would be able to help him. And the Cat knew where to find him.

The woods were lovely, dark, and deep, and with promises of revenge to keep, the Cheshire Cat walked toward the brick house. The war had raged for decades. Wolf would occasionally leave the brick house to haunt some poor, unsuspecting little girl or boy, usually on the way to their grandmother's or memere's or whathaveyou, usually with a basket full of food (though once there was a girl who carried a basket full of marijuana and another with crystal meth in it—boy had *that* been a party) but most of the time he was at the brick house stalking the last pig.

The light of the full moon broke through the opening where the intelligent porker had built his humble abode. Ivy grew up the side of the house. It'd been years since this tirade had begun. The pig's brothers had been eaten quickly, but this one, always the smart one, had survived. The Wolf was smarter than the other two pigs, but not this one. That could prove good for the cat.

He circled the clearing, picking up the Wolf's scent and followed it. He knew the Wolf could smell him, too, and that was fine.

The sensation came so quickly that the Cat couldn't leap out of the way in time. The Wolf's sharp teeth sank into his back (the teeth had been going for his neck, but the cat moved fast enough to miss *that* particular horror) and white-hot pain tore through the Cat. He screeched and hissed as the Wolf whipped his head from side to side. The Cheshire Cat's spine snapped and he lost all feeling in his lower quarters.

Motherfucker! he thought. *Here goes life number—*

And everything went black.

Through a dark darker than night,
The Cheshire Kitty Cat flew with fright.
He had lost life #7.
His mind had gone out
But there'd be no heaven.

His soul flowed, growing evermore black,
And the cat realized he was coming back
To the world he knew.
This was evident
By the light that was blue—

Why the light was always blue, the Cheshire Cat didn't know, nor did he really care. What he cared about was that he was back, that he had only two lives left, and that the Wolf stood over him, glaring with yellow eyes and allowing drool to drip on the Cat's head.

He's gone mad, the Cat thought. *All these years waiting for the pork chop have driven him absofuckinglutely* mad.

"Now, meow-meow," the Wolf said, and his lips pulled back into a grin that revealed long, sharp teeth. "I'm wondering what's brought your self-serving kitty ass over here. I know you're not going to visit the pig—you haven't visited him in years—so I'm wondering what you want with me."

"I—"

"Be quick," the Wolf interrupted. "You have twenty seconds before I eat you."

"I need some help with a rat bastard."

"A rat bastard? A rat with no father or someone who has crossed your path."

"Someone who's crossed my path."

"Ah," the Wolf said. "And they say crossing a *black* cat's path is bad luck. Now, say that I help you—not that I'm going to, I don't know exactly who you want taken down or how dangerous it could be—but say I help you. What's in it for me?"

"Oh," the Cheshire Cat said and grinned. "A tasty, tasty meal and the good tidings of..."

And that was how the Big Bad Wolf and the Cheshire Cat teamed up and got to following Brad, Gretchen, the Scarecrow, and the White Rabbit.

XIV
BRAD'S IMAGINATION & THE ATTACK

That feeling that something was watching them, following them, *stalking* them only grew stronger. As they walked along the path, the White Rabbit talked the whole time about its very large family (after all, it *was* a rabbit) and how this uncle and that aunt betrayed the others and this cousin was a devil weed addict and this cousin had become obsessed by a gold ring and that sister was a whore while this brother was... And it went on and on, and Brad blocked the words out with his own thoughts at some point. Besides talking almost nonstop, the other thing the White Rabbit did that became annoying very quickly was checking its pocket watch. Repeatedly checking the watch. But Brad did his best to leave these annoyances by losing himself in his own mind.

In the Real World, he was Brad Gautreau, the child of Randall and Patrice Gautreau, living in Harden, Massachusetts. When he used his imagination as a child he was an adventurer, a star pilot, a knight, a hero. The fantasies often grew more complex and they not only were an escape from the mundane, but an escape from preadolescent and adolescent torture. The way his classmates would get on his case for being quiet, for being smart. He'd been able to escape their slings and arrows by losing himself, by creating fantasy adventures or musing over dreams or incidents in his life. It had become the foundation of his writing. His imagination gave him anything he wanted. Even Miranda.

He envisioned her and him on a hill overlooking an ocean. The sunset painted the world pink and a nice breeze ruffled the grasses on the hill. Miranda, dressed in a pale yellow dress that was soft, relaxed, and stunning, reached out and touched his cheek. She smiled and leaned closer and closer until—

Silence.

Brad looked at the White Rabbit. It'd stopped talking. It'd stopped walking. Gretchen and the Scarecrow looked at the Rabbit, eyes wide with concern.

"What—?" Brad started.

"Shhh!" the White Rabbit hissed. Its ears stood almost straight up, and its whiskers twitched. Its red eyes scanned the trees around them. These woods weren't nearly as thick as the woods on the other side of the kingdom had been and hiding would not be as easy for their stalker—for Brad was sure that's what the Rabbit had heard.

"We're being followed," the White Rabbit said, voice low. Again, the whiskers twitched, followed by the ears. "There are two of them." It gulped. "And they're *hungry*."

That's when a wolf howled and all hell broke loose.

Something invisible crashed through the leaves from the lower branches of a tree to the left of the road. The White Rabbit went down fighting. Brad had begun to rush over to help it (several cuts had already opened in places on the Rabbit's arms and white fur instantly became red in places) when a large wolf crashed down through the rattling leaves of trees to the right of the road. It landed in front of Brad and swung a claw. Brad leapt back, the sharp nails just missing, and his heel struck a rock. The wolf swung again, missing again, though this time it was because Brad had fallen on his back. Gretchen screamed. The wolf lifted its head and howled.

The howl sank into the lowest places in Brad's stomach and chilled him. He wished he'd thought to borrow Jack and Jill's double-barreled shotgun. How could he have been so stupid not to? He noticed that he'd stumbled over a rock as big as a grapefruit.

"Now," the Wolf said, looming over Brad with drool dangling from its lower jaw. "Time to eat."

At that moment, the still-invisible Cheshire Cat let out a piercing shriek as the Scarecrow grabbed it off the White Rabbit, swung, and threw it. It became visible as it sailed through the air, twisting and landing on its feet with a hiss. The Rabbit hopped to its feet.

The Wolf glanced back at the ruckus, and Brad used the moment to grab the rock that he'd stumbled over. The Wolf turned back to Brad and dived at him. Gripping the cold rock, Brad swung with all his strength and felt a drop of drool hit his forehead. It connected with the Wolf's muzzle with a crunch. Blood spurted from its black nose and it moved away from Brad, whining.

"You *fuck!*" the Wolf bellowed. "I'm gonna gut you like a fish."

Gretchen dropped to her knees behind the backpedaling Big Bad Wolf, and hunched over. The Wolf backed into her and stumbled, falling back. Gretchen rolled away from the monster, who was already beginning to get to its feet. Brad, now on his feet, rushed over with the rock, rage engulfing him, and brought it down on the Wolf's head with a dull thud-crack. The Wolf's yellow eyes rolled up and it fell back.

Good, the voice said. *Grasp onto your anger and* use *it*.

Brad turned and saw that the Cheshire Cat had gone invisible again. The Scarecrow walked in a circle looking for it. The White Rabbit did the same, listening, ears twitching. Gretchen, too, was on her feet.

"He's still here," the White Rabbit whispered. "I can hear him. I can smell him."

"You might be able to smell me," the Cheshire Cat said, its mouth becoming visible on the ground near the White Rabbit. "But I'm going to *taste* you!"

It attacked, burying its teeth into the White Rabbit's flesh. The Scarecrow rushed in again and its knee popped, spraying straw every which way, and its leg buckled backwards. The Scarecrow fell and four new lines ripped open on its face, spilling more straw.

Rock still in hand and adrenaline mixed with rage, mad rage, flowing through Brad's bloodstream, he rushed to the nearly invisible cat (its eyes had now joined its mouth as being the only visible parts of it) and brought the rock down on its head. The Cat hissed and four slits opened on the back of his hand. The pain only fueled Brad's rage further and everything blinked out as he brought the rock down again. The White Rabbit scrambled back.

"You fucker!" the Cat screamed. "I'll kill y—"

The rock took out the Cat's teeth. It blinked fully back into existence and tried to scramble away but Brad held it down with his left hand, ignoring the scratches, and brought the rock down again and again. Each thud of the rock hitting the oversized cat's skull brought a tiny, minute sense of relief. Finally, the Cheshire Cat stopped struggling, its face crushed under the rock's repeated bashing.

Brad almost thought he heard the voice laughing, but chalked it up to adrenaline and imagination. He dropped the bloody rock and fell away from the dead cat. His body trembled and he breathed heavily. His heartbeat filled his ears and he felt spent, the ejaculation of his rage leaving him woozy and nauseated. He became aware of his companions staring at him. The Scarecrow's face needed stitches, as did its left knee (which it bent to hold closed) but its painted eyes were on Brad, its body rigid with shock (and possibly fear?). Gretchen also looked at him and her brown eyes were wide, and he knew fear filled them. The White Rabbit also stared at him, its red eyes not wide. It simply nodded.

"You may not be *him*," it said. "But you're not far removed."

"Who?" Brad said, a little surprised his voice was there to be used.

The Rabbit shook its head. "It's not important. We should stick around in case *he*—" It nodded to the dead cat. "—comes back again. We don't know which life of his nine he was on."

Brad shook his head as he stood. "I'm not killing him again. At least not right now. If he comes back again, maybe he'll be smart enough not to make me kill him a third time."

"Yes," the White Rabbit said. "Maybe." It didn't sound convinced.

XV
THE CAT'S LAST LIFE & THE SHACK

The rat bastard, the Cheshire Cat thought as the blue light brought him back from the black. *I can't believe he fucking killed me again.*

His mouth ached as teeth grew back. His whole face throbbed as it rebuilt itself. He hissed and meowed, unable to control himself; the pain was too much. Soon, though, he was rebuilt and the pain was nothing more than a faint echo. He rose, stretched, and saw the Big Bad Wolf. The rat bastard had killed him, too. The bloody rock that had done in both of them lay on the dirt path. The Cat slinked over to the Big Bad Wolf.

"Not so big and bad, huh?" he said. Then he began eating the Wolf. Why let the Wolf's death be for nothing? The least a kitty could do was allow his acquaintance's death not to be completely in vain.

"Nourish me," the Cat said. "And hopefully your stupidity won't infiltrate my bloodstream. After all, that fucking pig hasn't lived in the brick house for years. He built a tunnel and left it *ages* ago."

He chuckled and ate the Big Bad Wolf.

Once satisfied that the Scarecrow's straw wouldn't fall out of its torn leg, they picked their pace up and followed the path.

"She went this way, oh yes," the White Rabbit said. "I can trace her scent. Oh yes. Alice came this way."

The path wove through the woods and into a field. The sun moved across the sky and they picked berries for lunch. The White Rabbit knew which berries were good to eat and which would cause bellyaches (or worse, the rabbit took great delight in warning them). The afternoon passed and the White Rabbit talked more. At some point the Scarecrow took up the talking. Of course, its depression made them depressed, but in a way, it was better than the White Rabbit's machine-gun-paced inanities.

At some point, Gretchen began singing in a soft voice only she could hear and ignored the grown-ups.

The path stopped at a small wood shack. It looked like a shed. The boards were old and gray, weather-beaten.

"What now?" Gretchen asked.

Brad shrugged and went around the shack, but the path had run its course. When he came back to the front, Gretchen, the Scarecrow, and the White Rabbit looked at him.

"The road ends here," he said.

"You mean…it just *stops*?" the White Rabbit said.

"That's stupid," Gretchen said.

"So now what?" asked the Scarecrow.

The shack's door had a rusted latch holding it closed.

"I guess we see what's inside."

And Brad opened the door.

XVI

INSIDE THE SHACK & THE SHRINK DRINK

Behind the shack's door was a corridor that seemed to go on infinitely. If there was an end to the corridor, it was very, very far away; much farther away than the shack's depth should allow. Doors lined each side of the corridor. Light sconces jutted from the wall between each door and directly below the sconces, candles burned atop small tables, providing dimmer light.

"I've never seen *this* before," the White Rabbit said. "Actually, I've never really been beyond the Castle of Hearts." It then turned and sniffed the air.

"That cat's back."

Gretchen looked up at Brad, frightened.

"Come on," he said.

He took Gretchen's hand and entered the shack. The Scarecrow and the White Rabbit followed, closing the door behind them. Brad didn't think closing the door would stop the Cheshire Cat, but what the hell? Curiouser things had happened.

Each door was different. The doorjambs were intricately carved: some with Victorian designs, some modern, some alien. Doors were oak, plastic, stone, and metal. Plastic beads dangled in one doorway and when Brad peeked in, he saw a dark room with a woman dressed like a Gypsy sitting before a table with a glass ball. She sat alone and stared into the ball, which actually showed something that scared the woman. In that instant Brad picked up her thoughts:

It's real, she thought. *I don't believe it. All those people I've conned and this bloody thing* really *works!*

Then she lifted her head and stared at another door covered by multicolored plastic beads.

"There is two of him," she said. "It will be messy."

Someone tugged Brad's jacket and he came back into the corridor. The Scarecrow looked at him, its painted eyes unchanged but its body language quite serious. "That's not where you're supposed to be."

"How do you know?" Brad asked. "With all these doors, how *can* you know?"

The Scarecrow shrugged. "It doesn't make sense. We'll know your door when we find it."

They continued along the corridor, passing door after door. One door was painted white with the brass number 217 on it. One doorway had elevator doors. One was made from raw wood and had 19 carved into it. The travelers walked in silence. The White Rabbit didn't tell any of its stories about its extremely large family. The Scarecrow didn't complain or wallow. Gretchen grasped Brad's hand, seeking comfort like the scared little girl she actually was and providing comfort at the same time.

Brad's mouth was dry. Had Miranda come through here? If so, which door had she gone through? Had she chosen the correct one?

"Here," Scarecrow said.

"It has to be," Gretchen agreed.

The door and doorjamb were wood and painted white. No intricate carvings. No doorknob. Just plain.

"Why this one?" Brad asked.

"It's the only one without a design," Scarecrow said. "It sticks out."

Brad noticed that its plainness did indeed draw more attention to the door. He nodded, took a deep breath, and went to the door. He pushed it open a crack and peered through.

A man sat hunched over a notebook computer, the same kind Brad owned. He stared at the screen, fingers tapping frantically at the keys. He wore glasses and music played from connected stereo speakers. He had brown hair and a few moles on the side of his face that Brad could see. He looked quite a bit like Brad—too much like him, actually. The man was completely unaware of him. This couldn't be the right door. Brad squinted and looked at the notebook computer's screen.

The man wrote: Brad squinted and looked at the notebook computer's screen.

Brad gulped and pulled back into the corridor, closing the door.

"That's not the right door," he said.

"How do you know?" Scarecrow asked. "It *has* to be the right one."

"It's not," Brad said. He sighed and shook his head. "I don't know what—" He stopped.

"What?" asked Gretchen.

"That."

On the table across from them, along with the candle, was a bottle with a wineglass. A small card sat on the table in front of the bottle and read—

Drink me.

Brad approached the table.

A bang came from down the corridor, from the direction they'd come. They couldn't have come a mile, could they? It appeared so. They may have come even more than a mile from the shack's door to the plain white door. White light came from the distant, open door, and something slinked in.

"The Cat," the White Rabbit said, voice soft and shaky.

"Drink it," the Scarecrow said. "Now, and find the door. I'll stop the cat."

"But you have to come with us," Gretchen said.

The Scarecrow shook its head. "I can't. I can't drink that. I don't have a real mouth or a throat or a stomach. I'll hold the Cat back and try to take another of its good-for-nothing lives. You three go on."

The Cat raced down the hall at an absurd speed.

"*Now!*" the Scarecrow yelled.

Brad opened the bottle and poured some clear, pink liquid into the glass. He brought the drink up and its scent infiltrated his nostrils. Not a bad scent, pleasing. He drank and handed the glass to Gretchen. She drank and passed the glass to the White Rabbit, who drank down the last gulp.

It placed the glass on the table and looked at Brad and Gretchen. "Now what?"

At that moment, tingling exploded through Brad's body, similar to what had happened when they'd eaten the scones and mushroom. The corridor's dimensions changed. They were shrinking again.

"Be safe," the Scarecrow said.

At that moment, the Scarecrow flew back, attacked by an invisible force. Straw flew into the air as its chest tore open.

Brad, Gretchen, and the White Rabbit stopped shrinking. Brad guessed he was no more than four inches tall, the size of an action figure.

"Look!" Gretchen said, pointing to something under the table.

Brad turned and saw a door that was the perfect size for them. They hadn't noticed it before because it was small and under the table. But this, indeed, was the door meant for him.

For *Brad* was carved into the wood.

The Cheshire Cat's hiss almost knocked Brad over and did knock Gretchen down. Two yellow eyes with black slits materialized in the air above them, followed by the smiling, deadly mouth. The cat laughed.

"Gotcha!" it said.

The White Rabbit's chest opened, spurting blood. The force of the blow from the Cat's invisible claw took it off its big feet. It was dead before the Cheshire Cat ate it.

"One down," the Cat purred. "Two to—"

At that moment, the Scarecrow grabbed the Cheshire Cat by the scruff of its neck and yanked it from the floor. The Cat materialized, twisting, hissing, meowing, growling, and slashing. Straw flew as the Scarecrow reached for the candle that sat on the tabletop.

"Why won't you die?" the Scarecrow yelled and jammed the burning candle against the cat.

The Cat screamed and its fur caught fire. It turned, a claw knocking the candle from Scarecrow's hand. The candle toppled to the floor and its flame ignited the dry straw sticking out between Scarecrow's leg and foot. The Scarecrow went up instantly.

Gretchen screamed as the flaming Cat fell to the floor, making unearthly sounds. The Scarecrow dropped and rolled on the carpet to no avail.

The burning cat looked at Brad and Gretchen. "Oh, no you don't!" it hissed. "This is my last life and I'll be damned if you get away!"

It lurched toward Brad and Gretchen and they leaped back. Brad closed his eyes, ready for the agony that would surely come as the cat's claw tore through his body, but no pain came, just the horrible scent of burning straw, cloth, meat, and wood, and the sounds of struggling along with the hot wind as fire came close and then was pulled away. He opened his eyes to see that the Scarecrow had grabbed the Cat by the tail. Its burning arm was being extended by the burning cat's frantic struggle to break loose, but the Scarecrow still managed to keep hold.

"Get out!" the Scarecrow screamed at Brad and Gretchen. "Get out *now!*"

The Cheshire Cat wasn't moving as much as it had been even moments before, but it still struggled as it died, intent on getting them. Brad grabbed Gretchen's hand and opened the small door with his name on it. They rushed through, closing the door behind them. A moment later something thumped against it and let out a long, agonizing mewl.

Smoke sifted through the crack between the door and its jamb, but soon stopped. The door itself faded into the molding on the wall.

"Where are we?" Gretchen asked, studying their new environment.

Brad turned and his heart leaped into his throat. It looked odd from this height, but he recognized his apartment immediately. Directly in front of him were two six-foot bookcases that looked like skyscrapers from this size. He looked up at them, getting the same sense of vertigo he got when he visited Boston or New York, cities he had dreamed of living in, once upon a time.

On the top shelf, standing between Darth Vader and Luke Skywalker action figures, was an action figure he'd never seen before.

That's no action figure, he thought. *That's* Miranda!

Even from this distance he could tell. She wore a pale yellow dress with a white apron. Her auburn hair was held back by a white headband.

"Is that Alice on the shelf?" Gretchen asked. "Are we going up there?"

"Yes and yes," Brad said and headed for the bookcase.

XVII
UP THE BOOKCASE & JABBERWOCKY

B rad and Gretchen walked across the floor (what would have been less than a step at their normal sizes was a short walk for them now) and climbed onto the bottom shelf. Paperback and hardcover books stood taller than the two of them. Sounds came from the books. As they climbed up to the next shelf, the roaring of a river came from *The Adventures of Huckleberry Finn*. Brad pulled himself onto the next shelf and helped Gretchen up after him. The smell of dust emanated from Steinbeck's *The Grapes of Wrath* and a single, terrible gunshot came from *Of Mice and Men*.

Tell me about the rabbits, George, said the voice in Brad's mind. It seemed stronger, even more of a separate entity than it was before.

Brad and Gretchen climbed the books from one shelf to the next, slowly working toward the top, toward Miranda. Halfway up the bookcase, a roar came from above and Miranda's voice from the top shelf followed.

"Beware the Jabberwock!" she yelled.

At that moment, a large creature crawled down from the shelf above them. Its eyes of flame locked on them and it roared, its large jaws opening wide enough to fit Brad between them, standing. Its massive claws let go of the shelf and wings flapped, keeping it hanging in the air.

"Jubjub bird!" Gretchen screamed.

The claws swung out, trying to catch them, and Brad grabbed Gretchen's arm and jumped off the books. The Jabberwock's tail swung around and hit Brad in the chest. He flew back, crashing into Orwell's *1984*. Gretchen ran and climbed up a stack of Joyce Carol Oates books, and grabbed the next shelf. She pulled herself up and disappeared.

"Come 'n get me!" she screamed.

The manxome foe looked down at Brad, then up at Gretchen, indecisive. It decided to go after the smaller prey first, and flapping its wings, began to rise. Brad ran and jumped, grabbing onto the Jabberwock's tail.

The Jabberwock, the Jubjub bird, the frumious Bandersnatch—whatever you preferred to call it—roared and whipped its tail. Brad hugged it, holding on as well as he could and fought the dizziness that came with so much tossing. Eventually he could no longer hold on and flew onto the shelf with Gretchen. She clutched a sword. Brad didn't know where the sword came from.

"Come on!" Gretchen screamed. "I'll take your head!"

The Jabberwock's claw grasped Gretchen and lifted her toward its large mouth. Brad ran to fight it, but again, the tail whipped at him and he crashed into the books. She slashed the vorpal blade—*snicker-snack!*—through the claw. The beast let out an ear-piercing shriek as its claw fell to the floor many stories down. Gretchen clutched the beast's arm and climbed up the hovering monster, onto its back between its wings.

"Go get Alice," she yelled to Brad, then turned her attention to the Jabberwock. "This is for Hansen, you brillig bozo! Callooh! Callay!"

She swung the vorpal blade and one of the Jabberwock's wings fell off, then the blade sliced through the other one. As the beast fell, Gretchen brought the blade down and through the top of the monster's skull.

Brad's heart leapt into his throat and lead filled his stomach as he watched Gretchen and the Jabberwock fall down, down, down to the floor. The Jabberwock was dead before it landed. The sound of Gretchen hitting the floor came back to Brad moments after he saw it. Her small body lay broken on the floor. In the end, she'd shown more guts than Brad would ever possess. His heart ached and tears made the world shimmer.

Alone now. He hadn't realized how much his companions had helped him through this. But that was what it always came to, wasn't it? In the end, you have to go alone.

One shelf remained to be conquered. Miranda was there. *Alice*, as his companions and the others of this world insisted on calling her. Brad stood on rubbery legs and climbed to the top shelf.

XVIII

ALICE & THE MAD HATTER

B rad needed three shelves for his Stephen King collection. The last of the books were on this top shelf, including *The Dark Tower* books. *Star Wars* action figures lined the shelf in front of the books. Young Obi-Wan Kenobi stood near old Obi-Wan "Ben" Kenobi, both holding clear blue plastic lightsabers. Near him was young Anakin Skywalker as a Jedi Knight, a clear blue plastic lightsaber in a black-gloved, robotic hand. Darth Vader stood beside his former self, grasping clear red plastic for his lightsaber. Lastly, Luke Skywalker was dressed in his black *Return of the Jedi* outfit, holding his green lightsaber. On the edge of the shelf, legs dangling over, smoking a cigarette, sat Miranda.

Her *Alice's Adventures in Wonderland* getup was a little messy; some dirt (and perhaps blood) was smeared on the apron. If she'd had to go through the things he had, she was lucky that's all that clung to her clothes. Seeing her there alive, all right, and looking somewhat pissed off, his heart leapt and he went to her.

"Miranda," he said. "Oh, Christ, I'm so glad you're all right."

She took a final drag of her cigarette and crushed it out on the shelf. "Of course I'm all right," she said. "Why wouldn't I be?" She got to her feet and looked at him.

Brad wanted to take her, hold her, kiss her all over...feel her to make sure she was real.

"I've been so scared," he said. "When I went to your house and you weren't there I thought you might be in trouble."

Miranda shook her head. "I'm not in trouble. At least, nothing I can't handle. Why are *you* here?"

Brad blinked. Hadn't he made it obvious? "I wanted to make sure you were okay."

"Why else?" Her blue eyes were unblinking. They looked into him, seemingly studying more than just his face, appearing to sink beneath his flesh and into his soul.

"What do you mean?" he asked.

"You know what I mean," Miranda said. "There's another reason you're here. What is it?"

She looked over the edge. He did, too. The broken Jabberwock and little girl lay far, far below. He looked at Miranda.

"To rescue you," he said, voice barely above a whisper. "I wanted to rescue you."

"From what?"

The words could have been a slap.

"Brad," Miranda said. "What do I need rescuing from?"

Brad opened his mouth but nothing would come.

"I don't need to be rescued from anything," she said. "Thank you...but no thank you. I'm fine."

Then came laughing. A man sat on the top of *The Green Mile's* binding. He wore a purple suit and a large top hat. His head was back, hands clutching the top of the bookbinding and legs kicking in hysterics.

"Oh, shit," the man said, and the voice sounded familiar to Brad. Too familiar. Goosebumps prickled over his body. "Aw, fuck. That's *classic!*"

The Mad Hatter pushed himself off the book and landed on the shelf.

"I think, my dear," the Mad Hatter said, head down and the hat covering his features, "he means he wants to save you—" Brad didn't want to see to whom the voice, which had provided sarcastic commentary since he'd awakened at two in the morning the night before, belonged. "—from *me.*"

The Mad Hatter looked up and Brad, with a chill that rattled him, looked at his own face.

XIX

MIRANDA & BRAD

Brad stared at himself dressed in the clothes of the Mad Hatter.

"Some hero *you* are," the doppelganger (the Brad Hatter?) said. "Did you *really* think you could rescue her?"

"He's right," Miranda said. "I don't need to be rescued."

The Brad Hatter looked at her.

"Why so surprised?" Miranda said. "You don't think I could've left before now?" She looked at Brad. "You needed to see this for yourself. You need to take care of it."

"No." The Brad Hatter shook his head. "You're not going anywhere. You *have* to stay here."

"That's what you said when you put me over there," Miranda said, pointing over to the wall where the doorway had been.

Brad saw a pedestal standing against the wall. It went up to what would normally be his waist. Its dark wood was intricately carved and red silk lined the top. Brad had never seen it before.

"It's perfect for her," the Brad Hatter said, voice soft and devoid of any madness for the moment. "Isn't it?"

Brad could only nod.

"I don't belong on a pedestal," Miranda said with a sigh. "You need to sort this out, Brad." She walked to the edge of the shelf. "I'll see you later."

"No!" both Brads yelled together. Fear entwined with Brad's voice, while desperation entwined in the Brad Hatter's.

Miranda looked Brad in the eye with an arched eyebrow and her sly, mischievous smile, and stepped off the shelf.

Brad and the Hatter rushed to the edge. Miranda dropped, and catching the air, her dress ballooned out. She slowly drifted toward the floor like Mary Poppins with her umbrella. Before she could land, a blue light engulfed her and she disappeared.

She hadn't needed to be rescued—she never had—but he'd never given her a chance to tell him because…

"You," the Hatter said.

Brad looked up into his own face. The Brad Hatter's face was rigid. He shook, fists clenched tight and eyes wild.

"It's *your* fault," the Brad Hatter said. "You turned her against me!"

Brad's heart rammed. He understood now. Of course. "Look, this is—"

"*The end!*" the Brad Hatter screamed.

He spun and grabbed the plastic red lightsaber out of the Darth Vader action figure's hand. A moment later, the plastic glowed and hummed. The Brad Hatter brought the lightsaber down and Brad ducked to the right, near the Luke Skywalker action figure. The glowing, humming red blade just missed him. The Brad Hatter screamed and swung the lightsaber, taking off Luke Skywalker's head. Luke fell back, his clear plastic stand still attached to his feet. Brad grabbed the green plastic lightsaber from his hand, clutching the silver-painted handle.

It has to change, he thought. *It has to become real.*

The Brad Hatter advanced and swung again. Brad brought the plastic lightsaber up and the red blade slashed through it, melting the points of the plastic it touched.

You just have to believe in yourself.

Brad blinked. Miranda had said that when they were at the beach, her Thinking Place, sitting in her car talking. He'd asked her what her dreams were.

I don't have many, she said. *That way, if they don't come true, I'm not hurt. What about you?*

I want to write, Brad had said. *I just want to write.* And love, he'd added silently. He wanted love.

Well, she'd said. *All you have to do is believe in yourself.*

The red blade swung low and Brad leapt, the blade cutting the air where his shins had been. He landed, spun, and ran toward the Anakin Skywalker action figure. He grabbed Anakin's blue plastic lightsaber. Holding the silver and black painted handle, Brad stared at the blade. The clear blue plastic began glowing and soon it hummed. The Brad Hatter attacked and Brad blocked every blow.

"There can only be one of us," the Brad Hatter said. "And *you're* not the one."

"Wrong," Brad said.

He pushed the Brad Hatter away and then held his arms out, closing his eyes. If he was wrong…

The Brad Hatter swung the lightsaber down in an arc and Brad prepared for the heat and pain to cut through him. It didn't though. Instead, plastic hit his shoulder and stopped. When he opened his eyes, the Brad Hatter looked at his clear red plastic lightsaber, frustration on his face.

"What the fuck?" he screamed.

Brad dropped his own toy lightsaber and grabbed the Brad Hatter by his lapels.

"Come on," Brad said, closed his eyes, and pulled the Brad Hatter off the edge of the shelf.

He hit the floor with a thud and opened his eyes. He was back to his normal size, five-ten. A moment later, the Brad Hatter's fist smashed into Brad's right cheek. Brad grabbed out, his hand falling on a leather-bound edition of *The Complete Works of Edgar Allan Poe*, a massive volume bought ten years before. The corner of the book came in handy when smashing the Brad Hatter's face, leaving a bloody gash above his right eye.

Brad stood. The Brad Hatter leapt to his feet and attacked. They crashed into the bathroom and the Brad Hatter grasped Brad's throat with both hands. He pushed Brad back hard, attempting to smash his head into the mirror, only Brad's head passed through the mirror as it might pass through a membrane. It tingled around his flesh. The Brad Hatter's face wavered on the other side of the mirror.

Surprised, the Brad Hatter loosened his grasp just a bit. But it was enough. Brad kicked his knee up, connecting with his doppelganger's stomach. The Brad Hatter let go of Brad, who climbed onto the sink, grabbed the doppelganger by the back of the neck, and then jumped through the looking glass.

The Brad Hatter screamed and struggled and held tight even after most of his body was through.

"No!" he screamed. "It *hurts!*"

Brad took a deep breath and made one last pull. The Brad Hatter lost his grip and both he and Brad fell back. Brad's head hit on the side of the tub and everything went black.

XX
BRAD

*W*here's *Miranda?* was Brad's first thought when his eyes popped open at 2:30 AM. He saw her in his mind's eye, standing on the edge of a bookshelf wearing a pale yellow dress with white apron, the gleam in her blue eyes and the sly grin on her pink lips.

There was the sense that something was wrong and his heart raced. He sat up in bed. For some reason, he thought that his head should hurt and he touched the back of it. He winced, expecting pain, and was surprised when there was none.

Miranda, a voice said. *You have to make sure she's okay.*

Brad got up and went to the phone. He was about to dial when he stopped. It was 2:30 in the morning. Why would he chance waking her up?

Because something's wrong, the voice pleaded. *Please. Call her and make sure everything's all right. Then we can go back to sleep.*

"No," Brad said and put the phone down.

He went into the bathroom, pissed, and went back to bed. As he drifted off to sleep, the voice (that for some reason made Brad think of a large, purple top hat) said, *You'll be sorry.*

Maybe, Brad thought. But he thought maybe he'd be sorrier if he called Miranda and woke her up just to make sure she was all right. Of course she was all right. If she wasn't, she'd let him know, and then he could be a hero. Being a hero wasn't just saving people but also knowing when to stand back.

Brad smiled. He thought that he may have an idea for a new story to write in the morning. His eyes closed and as he drifted off to sleep, he thought he heard distant laughter. But that was impossible, wasn't it?

That was simply mad.

AUTHOR'S NOTE

The initial drafts of this story were written during some tough times when many doubts swirled through my head. I'd like to take a moment to thank a few friends who encouraged me and gave me feedback.

There were several co-workers from my days as a bookseller at a local independent bookstore, to them I say thank you for your kind words and encouragement.

Thank you to Greg F. Gifune and Dawn Clifton Tripp, fellow wordsmiths from the South Coast area of Massachusetts, who took the time to read the novella and give encouragement.

Thanks to Roy and Liz at Bad Moon Books, who initially took a chance on this story.

Which leads me to John R. Little, because he not only took a chance to read an unpublished manuscript from a "new" writer, but was willing to vouch for it when he recommended that I submit it to Bad Moon Books.

Thanks are also in order to David Wilson and David Dodd for giving this story, like my version of the Cheshire Cat, another life.

Thanks to Kim Gatesman, a great artist and friend, for the kind words and advice on the story.

I also want to thank Maureen Lacasse, the greatest teacher I ever had, who has helped me many times and is a constant source of inspiration in my life, especially for the day job.

My mother, Pat, who read the manuscript and admitted that I'd done something—other than giving her a granddaughter—

right, died in February 2019. She'd be thrilled by this new edition. Also my father, Ray, deserves thanks for so much assistance that I'll never be able to fully pay back.

Of course, I *have* to thank my daughter, Courtney Elizabeth. When this book was originally published in 2011, she was probably embarrassed that I kept putting her name in print, though I believe she secretly thought it was cool. She's an adult now and embarking on her life journey, and maybe she'll read this and smile.

When this story was originally written and published, Genevieve wasn't born, but now I *have* to thank her for continuing to inspire me and always being ready to click *Submit* when I send in my work. She's too young to read this now, but someday….

Way back at the beginning, you saw that this story is dedicated to two friends:

Thanks, Michelle Marshall, without whom this book wouldn't exist. Be careful when you approach that rabbit hole.

Thank you *so* much to Toby Gray who, along with his wife Leslie, provided continuous support in every aspect of my life. Toby is one of my heroes.

And finally, I want to thank my wife, Pamela. I read this book to her aloud for over two-and-a-half hours in March 2007 and she has encouraged me ever since to find it a home, and to keep it out There. Not only did she encourage me, but she married me. I love you, babe. Your book is coming.

B.G.
November 30th, 2010
February 14th, 2021
Dartmouth, Massachusetts

Meet the Author

Bill Gauthier is the author of *Echoes on the Pond*, *Catalysts*, *Alice on the Shelf*, and *Shadowed*. His work has appeared in magazines and anthologies including *Dark Discoveries* and the award-winning *Borderlands* anthologies. He lives in Southeastern Massachusetts with wife and children. By day he teaches in a media-based technology program at a vocational-technical high school, where he helps teenagers find their voices and follow their dreams. By night, he writes dark stories, middle-grade space adventures, essays, blog posts, and generally skirts the edges of acceptability and rebellion.

Bibliography

Alice on the Shelf
Catalysts
Echoes on the Pond
Shadowed

Curious about other Crossroad Press books? Stop by our website: http://crossroadpress.com
We offer quality writing
in digital, audio, and print formats.

Subscribe to our newsletter on the website homepage and receive a free eBook.

www.ingramcontent.com/pod-product-compliance
Lightning Source LLC
Chambersburg PA
CBHW022039170626
46808CB00003B/1273